3 8015 00618 9264

KT-194-291

3 8015 00618 9264

SPECIAL MESSAGE TO READERS

This book is published under the auspices of

THE ULVERSCROFT FOUNDATION

(registered charity No. 264873 UK)

Established in 1972 to provide funds for research, diagnosis and treatment of eye diseases. Examples of contributions made are: —

A new Children's Assessment Unit at Moorfield's Hospital, London.

•

Twin operating theatres at the Western Ophthalmic Hospital, London.

•

A Chair of Ophthalmology at the University of Leicester.

•

The establishment of a Royal Australian College of Ophthalmologists "Fellowship".

You can help further the work of the Foundation by making a donation or leaving a legacy. Every contribution, no matter how small, is received with gratitude. Please write for details to:

**THE ULVERSCROFT FOUNDATION,
The Green, Bradgate Road, Anstey,
Leicester LE7 7FU, England.
Telephone: (0116) 236 4325**

**In Australia write to:
THE ULVERSCROFT FOUNDATION,
c/o The Royal Australian College of
Ophthalmologists,
27, Commonwealth Street, Sydney,
N.S.W. 2010.**

I've travelled the world twice over,
Met the famous: saints and sinners,
Poets and artists, kings and queens,
Old stars and hopeful beginners,
I've been where no-one's been before,
Learned secrets from writers and cooks
All with one library ticket
To the wonderful world of books.

© JANICE JAMES.

THE TWISTED SWORD

In 1815, the shadow of war reaches out even to the remote corners of Cornwall. For Ross and Demelza Poldark the year starts in Paris, with gaiety and laughter — but suddenly it turns to fearful separation, distrust and danger. Their elder son, Jeremy, is parted from his beloved wife, Cuby, to become a leader of men on the battlefield of Waterloo. For their daughter Clowance, and Stephen her husband, fate adds a sardonic twist to their hopes and plans. And always for Demelza there is the shadow of the secret she does not even share with Ross — the secret of the loving cup.

Books by Winston Graham
in the Charnwood Library Series:

STEPHANIE
THE TWISTED SWORD: PART ONE

WINSTON GRAHAM

THE TWISTED SWORD

PART TWO

A Novel of Cornwall
1815 – 1816

Complete and Unabridged

CHARNWOOD
Leicester

First published in Great Britain in 1990 by
Chapmans Publishers Limited
London

First Charnwood Edition
published June 1995
by arrangement with
Chapmans Publishers Limited
London

The right of Winston Graham to be identified as
the author of this work has been asserted by him
in accordance with the
Copyright, Designs and Patents Act, 1988

Copyright © 1990 by Winston Graham
All rights reserved

British Library CIP Data

Graham, Winston
    The twisted sword: part two.—Large print ed.—
Charnwood library series
I. Title II. Series
823.912 [F]

ISBN 0–7089–8828–8

CROYDON LIBRARIES

LIB   U   NO. 6189264

CLASS   F

V   ULV   P 15.95.

STK Published by   8 · 8 · 95

F. A. Thorpe (Publishing) Ltd.
Anstey, Leicestershire

Set by Words & Graphics Ltd.
Anstey, Leicestershire
Printed and bound in Great Britain by
T. J. Press (Padstow) Ltd., Padstow, Cornwall

This book is printed on acid-free paper

For
MAY

Deliver my soul from the sword;
my darling from the power of the dog.
Psalm 22: verse 20

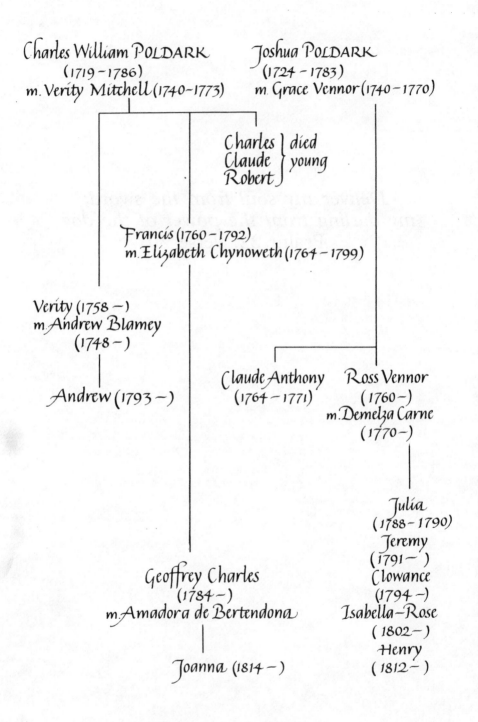

Charles William POLDARK
(1719–1786)
m. Verity Mitchell (1740–1773)

Joshua POLDARK
(1724 – 1783)
m. Grace Vennor (1740–1770)

Charles ⎫ died
Claude ⎬ young
Robert ⎭

Francis (1760–1792)
m. Elizabeth Chynoweth (1764 – 1799)

Verity (1758 –)
m. Andrew Blamey
(1748 –)

Andrew (1793 –)

Claude Anthony
(1764 – 1771)

Ross Vennor
(1760 –)
m. Demelza Carne
(1770 –)

Julia
(1788 – 1790)
Jeremy
(1791 –)
Clowance
(1794 –)
Isabella–Rose
(1802 –)
Henry
(1812 –)

Geoffrey Charles
(1784 –)
m. Amadora de Bertendona

Joanna (1814 –)

THE TWISTED SWORD

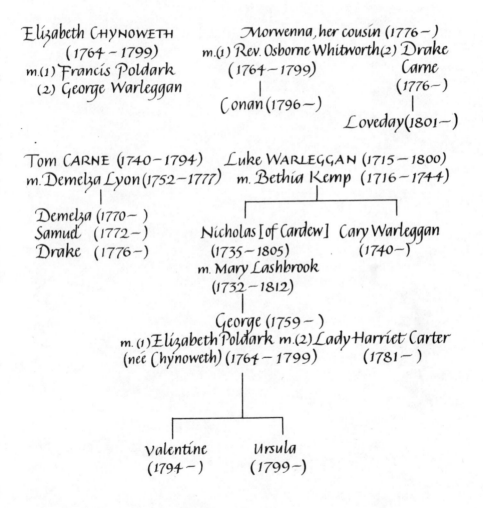

Elizabeth CHYNOWETH
(1764 – 1799)
m.(1) Francis Poldark
(2) George Warleggan

Morwenna, her cousin (1776 –)
m.(1) Rev. Osborne Whitworth (2) Drake
(1764 – 1799)   Carne
                                              (1776 –)
| |
Conan (1796 –)   Loveday (1801 –)

Tom CARNE (1740 – 1794)   Luke WARLEGGAN (1715 – 1800)
m. Demelza Lyon (1752 – 1777)   m. Bethia Kemp (1716 – 1744)
|
Demelza (1770 –)
Samuel (1772 –)   Nicholas [of Cardew] Cary Warleggan
Drake   (1776 –)   (1735 – 1805)   (1740 –)
                              m. Mary Lashbrook
                              (1732 – 1812)
                                       |
                              George (1759 –)
m. (1) Elizabeth Poldark   m.(2) Lady Harriet Carter
(née Chynoweth) (1764 – 1799)   (1781 –)

Valentine   Ursula
(1794 –)   (1799 –)

Book Three

1

LETTER from Ross Poldark to his wife, dated Brussels, 22nd June 1815.

Demelza,

I have to tell you that Jeremy is dead. I cannot bring myself to write the words, but there is no way I know of breaking this to you gently. He fell nobly and bravely in the great battle just fought in the area south of the village of Waterloo, about twelve miles from this city and won by the British and their Allies in a decisive manner that must finally and forever settle Bonaparte's fate.

I do not know, my dearest, how to begin to tell you what it has been like. In early June I escaped from internment in Verdun and tried to make my way towards Brussels. The difficulty of this journey, though little more than 150 miles, was far greater than the mere distance because between me and whatever troops defended Brussels lay the whole of the French army of the west — some 120,000 men. I was vastly lucky to avoid capture and probably would not have succeeded but for the help of a Colonel Colquhoun Grant, a British officer who was acting as a spy for Wellington, and between us, though we eventually travelled separately, we arrived at Wellington's headquarters as the main battle

*was about to begin. For the duration of
the battle Grant became one of the Duke's
aides-de-camp and I was invited to fulfil a
similar function. Naturally I tried to make
contact with Jeremy's regiment, but was sent
first with a message which took half the day,
partly because my horse was shot from under
me, though I escaped with a bruising.*

*The carnage on both sides was appalling.
I have never seen such ferocity in attack
or such utter relentless courage in defence.
Just around the farmhouse of Hougoumont,
which was where Jeremy was stationed, over
two thousand men were killed. In total we
are thought to have lost 20,000 men, the
Prussians about 7,000, the French about
30,000. Geoffrey Charles survived like me,
and did not even suffer a scratch, although he
was in the forefront of the fight throughout.
All Wellington's main aides were killed or
wounded — in total fifteen. Fitzroy Somerset
lost his right arm. Sir William de Lancey, the
Chief of Staff, was gravely wounded and is
not likely to recover. Adjutant General Barnes
and his deputy were both wounded. Colonel
Gordon and Colonel Canning both died. In
the battle the Duke of Brunswick died early,
and Lord Picton was killed on Sunday. Two
of Jeremy's closest friends were killed, and one
wounded. Young Christopher Havergal, who
made such a fuss of Bella, has lost a leg.
I have also just heard that Brigadier Gaston
Rougiet, who visited me in internment and
gave me a greater liberty which enabled me*

to escape, was killed at the very last, fighting the Prussians.

If there was ever a battle fought as savagely as this, I have never known it or want to hear of it.

They say that Fitzroy Somerset suffered the amputation of his arm without a murmur and that the next morning was seen to be practising writing with his left hand.

Dearest, dearest Demelza, I give you all these details not because they can interest you but because they keep me a little longer from the sort of detail that I find it so hard to face. Jeremy died a brave soldier's death; he led his much-depleted company against a French infantry brigade which outnumbered him ten to one. Because of the loss of my horse I was tardy in returning the message I carried to the Duke — who in extraordinary fashion survived the whole battle unscathed — but as soon as I had done this I hurried down towards where I knew Jeremy's company had been fighting all day. I arrived just as a Lieutenant Underwood was carrying him back after he had been shot.

He lived for perhaps half an hour, but did not seem to be in pain. He knew me and sent a loving message to you. That is all I can say.

That night, the Sunday night, I stayed by him, while the French army finally broke and then was utterly destroyed by the Prussians. I did a little to help some of the wounded but am afraid I was too distracted and distraught to have done all I should. On the Monday morning I was able to find a conveyance of a sort to carry him back to Brussels. The road was almost impassable still, for the wounded, the baggage trains, the commissary wagons, the medical supplies, wandering groups of soldiers trying to regain their units; we went with the majority, but a few vehicles were fighting their way against the tide. The road had almost broken up with the pressure it had been under and in some places was a sea of mud. In one place we were held up for fifteen minutes while vehicles were at a standstill. Then, sitting there as I did helpless upon my horse, I heard a voice cry 'Captain Poldark!'

It was Cuby. It seems that Lady de Lancey, Sir William's wife, hearing that her husband was lying grievously wounded in a cottage in the village of Waterloo, had hired a coach and coachman, and, learning of this, Cuby had asked if she might travel with her to see if she could gain news of Jeremy. It was my appalling duty to give her that news.

Dearest Demelza, I have never seen a woman more heartbroken than Cuby was when she realized what I was saying — I know of only one who will be more so and she is holding this letter. What can I say to comfort you when there is no comfort? I try to think of the three children we have left and our duty to them not to fall into utter despair. That many a father and mother through the ages have suffered as we suffer now does not *make it easier to sustain. Nor the thought of the thousands of other parents who have been bereaved by this battle. Perhaps we have always been too close a family. To feel so deeply about one's children is a great happiness — and a great danger.*

Jeremy is buried in the Protestant Cemetery of St Josse ten Noode, just on the south side of the Chausée de Louvain. It was a simple ceremony but a dignified one. A stone will be put up.

I am returning to England tomorrow with Cuby. She rode in front of me to Brussels, and I thought every moment she would faint and fall. I will remain a day or two in London before returning to Cornwall. At present she thinks she will stay a little while with her brother Augustus in London. She thinks that returning to Cornwall only seven months after leaving it in such happiness is more than she can face.

She bears our first grandchild.

My love, it is only three months since we separated but it is like an age. I long to see you. Perhaps we can comfort each other.

Ross

★ ★ ★

When Clowance heard she left a scribbled message on the kitchen table for Stephen — who had still not returned from his foray — and rode across to be with her mother. Verity went with her. Demelza's two brothers

7

were nearby — Drake at Trenwith, Sam at Pally's Shop. Dwight and Caroline too. Ben was at the mine and all the miners who had known and liked Jeremy so well. Paul and Daisy Kellow, with Mr and Mrs Kellow in the background; Valentine and Selina, just returned from Cambridge; the villagers from all the hamlets around. Letters began to arrive from as far afield as the Harveys at Hayle. A strange, stilted, troubled one from Cuby's mother. So many letters from people in the county: the Devorans, the Falmouths, the Trenegloses, the de Dunstanvilles, the Foxes. Even Harriet Warleggan sent a kind little note. Letters, letters; everyone so kind made the heartache worse.

Demelza took to walking across the beach and back, not to get rid of the deadly sickness and the emptiness and the aching — for there was no way out of that — but simply to tire one's muscles, to exhaust one's body, so that something was registered on the mind besides grief. Dwight gave her tincture of laudanum at night, but it always wore off at dawn when life was at its lowest and coldest.

Then she would stand by the window and cry alone for the loss of her son.

Verity did not like walking as far as the Dark Cliffs, but Clowance kept her mother company, most of the way in silence. When it was not Clowance, Drake would go, or sometimes Sam, though he had to be careful not to speak too much of God. Dwight told Demelza to go easy; twice Caroline persuaded her to visit Killewarren and spent part of the day with her.

It was almost only to Caroline that she found she could talk at all — and sometimes in the evening to Verity.

All the beauty had gone from Demelza's face. Perhaps one day it would return, but at present few of her friends in Paris would have taken her for the vivacious, comic, ebullient young woman they had known in February and March.

"Why have I so much cause to be bitter?" she said to Caroline once. "Folk die all the time — babies, old people, even young people like Jeremy. But I *am* bitter just the same. I don't want to see anyone, talk to anyone, be friendly with anyone. I just want to be left alone to think — to grieve — to think."

"My dear, that'll do you no good. Though I well comprehend — "

"It does good to remember," Demelza said. "It does good to remember a thousand days of caring . . ."

★ ★ ★

But, returning to the county more quickly than his old enemy, came Sir George Warleggan, full of the greatest satisfaction. For on careful calculation he decided that he had added twenty-four and a half per cent to his fortune. His belief that the Rothschilds would know first, and his commission to Rosehill to keep the closest watch on them and to make all the use he could of his friend in the Rothschild office — this had been triumphantly successful. Hardly eating a proper meal for three days, he had haunted the city and the Exchange. The nervousness of the early part of the week had intensified, and the market was like a sick patient with undulant fever, reacting to the lightest rumour.

Looking back on the situation as his personal coach carried him the last few miles through the thickly wooded valley towards his own home, he felt a supreme contempt for the way the government of the country had been run, the singular clumsiness of its communications, its total lack of any attempt to bridge more quickly the distance — at the most two hundred miles — between the House of Commons and the scene of an operation which would decide the fate of the world.

It seemed that the battle had raged for three days, from the 16th to the 18th June. It seemed that on Tuesday the 20th Mr Nathan Rothschild, by means of his swift-riding and swift-sailing couriers, had learned that there had been a victory for the Allied troops under the Duke of Wellington, and being on terms of the closest friendship with the British Government had informed them of this. The Cabinet, sitting in a sudden emergency session so early in the morning, had discounted the information as unfounded. Their own envoys had just brought them news of Quatre Bras, the British defeat and the retreat on Brussels. This had followed the news of the defeat of Blücher. The general opinion was that all was lost.

The same day in the afternoon a Mr Sutton, whose vessels plied between Colchester and

Ostend, had brought one of his ships back without waiting for passengers because he carried news of a tremendous battle being fought between Bonaparte and Wellington on the Sunday almost at the gates of Brussels. On the Wednesday *The Times* printed this information and wondered with regret that the Government had not made better arrangements for quicker transmission of the news. Were the Duke of Wellington's own despatches, the newspaper wondered, to depend upon similar vagaries of commercial patriotism? It was not until Thursday that the official bulletin was issued from Downing Street announcing the victory and calling Wellington the Hero of Britain.

But of course it had all happened for George on the Tuesday and Wednesday. Through his friend, Rosehill had been able to obtain the information that the Rothschilds had reported a victory for the Allies and that Downing Street had disregarded it. All that day George expected Nathan Rothschild to make some move. But when he did make a move, it was to sell stocks not to buy them . . . The market, already far down because of the news of Quatre Bras, fell still further. Not only George was watching the influential Jew.

George was puzzled, watchful, upset; for a while bitterly critical of Rosehill who he thought had given him wrong information. It's all over, said the brokers. And so did Rothschild's agents. The battle has been lost at a place called Waterloo. Rothschild, they said, has been hoodwinking the British Government.

Then Rosehill sidled up to George with a whispered comment: "The last hour of trading. Watch that."

In the last hour that the Exchange was open on the Wednesday Rothschild suddenly bought a huge parcel of shares, among them Consols, which had touched a new low. George, sweating heavily, immediately followed suit. He spent an unhappy morning on the Thursday when shares moved only erratically upwards, stimulated by a few people buying, including Rothschild again. Then the news of the great victory burst on the world — the French army utterly destroyed, Bonaparte making his escape to Paris, the Allies everywhere triumphant.

It was not only the Allies who were triumphant, George thought. Rothschild, by perfectly fair speculation, acting on the information he had already given the Government but which they had chosen to disregard, must have doubled his already immense fortune. And he, George, by astute emulation, had added about twenty-four and a half per cent to his already considerable fortune — or about eighty thousand pounds. It could have been more, he knew; but hedging at the last, still mindful of the disasters of 1810, and fearful of being cheated in some way by the cold young Jew, he had invested only two-thirds of what he might have done. Nevertheless, it was no mean achievement. Every night on the way home he had opened his business case, taken out a fresh piece of paper, and made his calculations afresh.

Just to complete the whole operation he had

sent Tankard flying back to Cornwall — more than post haste, killing his horses if necessary — with instructions to Lander to buy all the metals he could, chiefly copper, before anyone else knew of the victory. There was no assurance that the price of metals would go up as a result of Napoleon's defeat — might be the contrary — but if he could virtually corner the market he would be in a position to dictate its movements.

He looked forward to telling old Uncle Cary what he had done. Five years ago, Cary had been scathing in his denunciation of the speculation which hadn't come off. Now, though no doubt grumpy and grudging, as was his nature, he would have to admit the brilliance of the manoeuvre. Nothing spoke so convincingly to Cary as money.

George was also looking forward to seeing Harriet again. In the euphoria of Thursday he had bought her a present, a diamond brooch. It was second-hand and a bargain, but he had paid, if not more than its worth, more than he had intended, and occasionally this little worm of self-criticism came to disturb his sense of well-being. But at least Harriet, who loved jewellery, could not fail to be pleased.

He must be careful not to appear to boast to her about his coup; indeed he knew it would be better if he did not mention it at all — if he could *possibly* forbear. Harriet did not pretend to despise money — indeed, she liked it — but it was not central to her philosophy; it was only valuable to her for what it could buy;

and he knew if he told her of his successful speculation she would only congratulate him in an absent-minded way, looking cynically amused as she did so, and change the subject.

He wondered if Harriet had heard yet about Jeremy. The first casualty lists had been issued on the 4th July, and his name had been on it. George supposed the whole county would know about it now. Personally he was going to shed no tears; he never had liked the tall, gangling young buck: typical Poldark with his arrogance and his pride. The women were rather better — at least Clowance was — but the men were all the same. More fools they for going in the army and trying to be heroes. It seemed no time at all — though it was actually getting on for twenty years — since Ross himself had performed some so-called dare-devil rescue of Dwight Enys and others from a French prisoner-of-war camp and so had become a nine-days' wonder and the hero of the county. Well, now his son was gone, and bad luck for him and for his contriving a baronetcy for his son to inherit — though George had heard there was another son barely weaned yet; they bred like rabbits on the North Coast. That miner's brat with the stupid name; she'd had half a dozen at least.

But talking of breeding; there was his own wife pregnant now, bearing his son, who, with blue blood in his veins, would live to inherit all his mercantile wealth and possessions. What should they call him? George had a fancy for the name of Hector — or Nicholas; but no doubt Harriet would have ideas of her own.

He believed it would be about Christmas or January; Harriet was typically vague. It was still a long time to wait. Pray God the child wasn't premature . . .

The carriage turned in at the gates of Cardew, and George's eye looked about with critical appreciation, admiring the elegance and extent of his own property but scanning it for any evidence of indolence or neglect. When it came to the big pillared entrance of the mansion, one of the coachmen jumped down and opened the carriage door. At the same moment the door of the house opened and two footmen stood there to greet him. It was a warm afternoon and the coach had been stuffy — it needed to be well cleaned inside with a carriage soap and thoroughly brushed out.

He stretched his legs and his back, glad the journey was over, nodded to his servants and went into the hall. Harriet was crossing, followed by her two boarhounds. She looked up in surprise. Castor growled, and she put her hand on his muzzle to restrain him.

"Why, George," she said. "Good-day to you. You're soon back."

★ ★ ★

During the momentous days of late June, while the fate of empires was being decided, Stephen was cruising in the Channel hoping to settle some of the problems in his own life.

It seemed the *Adolphus* was out of luck. Fishing vessels and a few tiny trading

15

schooners — the latter just worth seizing but Stephen would not touch them; he was looking for bigger game. The weather was changeable, mainly sunny, almost calm; but then the wind would take off from an unexpected quarter and blow hard, so the crew was kept busy making and shortening sail. Twice they sighted larger vessels but Carter, who had been in the navy, was quick to recognize them as British warships. Then in a flurry of a brief squall they came suddenly in sight of a French frigate and had to run for their lives. The *Adolphus* crowded on all the sail she could and soon was heeling right over, white water along her lee rail, dipping and spouting into the short seas. It was an anxious two hours until nightfall.

Stephen had laid in a generous supply of stores: biscuit, beef, pork, peas, coffee, tea, sugar, flour, pepper, salt, lime juice; and he reckoned they had enough to last a good two weeks. Fresh water might force them in a bit earlier, but he began to hear rumblings of dissension among the crew. It was not, he discovered, discontent with his captaincy, but, with too much time on their hands, they were quarrelling among themselves.

Jason, who was his informant on most things, explained to him that there was a bitter rivalry between men from Falmouth and those from Penryn, and they were dividing into two camps with about a third of the crew uninvolved in either. One day Stephen heard a group of them shouting and jeering.

"Old Penrynners up in a tree," they shouted
"Looking as wisht as wisht can be.
Falmouth men be strong as oak
Can knock 'em down at every poke."

To which the men from Penryn shouted a more obscene rhyme back.

Looking at them, weather-beaten, long-nosed, hard-faced men, Stephen wondered that they could be such childish fools as to support a rivalry between two towns which were only a couple of miles apart. He'd been careful to lock up all the cutlasses and muskets he had brought and had appointed a man called Hodge as armourer.

Hodge was a little fat squab of a man, swart and jowly, but a bundle of energy and efficiency. Stephen soon saw him as the most valued member of the crew and began to consult him more and more. In his forty years he seemed to have done and been everything, and his experience as a sailor helped Stephen to fill the gaps in his own knowledge. Thank God he happened to come from St Ives.

But there was no knowing how many private knives were carried in secret places or how long it would be before the feud turned into a bitter battle. Jason also told him that they had brought rum aboard: he did not know where it was stored but some of the crew had access to it over and above the daily ration.

So it was a relief on the seventh day to sight what looked like a promising sail.

A beautiful still dawn, with a pearly sun

17

rising out of the early mists, turning them lemon-yellow and then to a grey scarf washed with scarlet. Yet as the sun rose it never came to full health. Anaemia set in, and the mist became light cloud chasing the colour from the sky. The gulls, which were always following *Adolphus*, rose and flapped and cried and settled again into the darkening water.

It was about noon that the look-out reported the sail. Stephen, who was not fond of heights, sent Carter up and then Jason. Soon you could see the sail from the deck.

"She's only got one mast," said Jason, disappointed, "but she's carrying a heavy sail."

Ten minutes later Carter came down. "Reckon tis a French chaloupe. She's just put out two headsails; means she's seen us and altered course."

The manoeuvring of the last few days had robbed Stephen of any idea where he really was, particularly as related to the French coast; but the drift of the *Adolphus* had been continually west, so it seemed likely that there was a great width of the Channel about them.

"Size is she?"

Carter pulled at his bottom lip. "Bigger'n you'd expect. A hundred ton maybe."

"Armed?"

"Likely."

"What with?"

"Could not say. Nothing big."

"Sure she's French?"

"Well, she's flying the French flag."

18

"Jason," said Stephen. "Go get the French flags. See if we can reassure her."

★ ★ ★

They pursued the *chaloupe* all day while the day went off. The sun disappeared about some other business, and cloud gathered and a light rain fell. It would have been impossible to keep the *chaloupe* in sight if the distance between them had not constantly lessened. Her captain clearly saw no reassurance in the flag Stephen flew and bore on a south-easterly course for home. But as the angle narrowed they overhauled him fast. Stephen ordered the armoury to be unlocked, and all men were issued with cutlasses or muskets. The sighting of a suitable prey had come just in time; the fraternal squabbling among the crew had ceased.

She was a strange-looking vessel to English eyes — very heavily sparred with an immense mainsail and a main boom very long and thick. She was steered by a long tiller, had high bulwarks and a wide stern. She should have been clumsy to handle, yet in fact moved well through the water and seemed to answer her helm readily. Her name, it seemed, was the *Revenant*.

Two of Stephen's six-pounders had been fitted as bow chasers, and when the distance warranted he told his gunners to try a shot or two in the hope of bringing down her mainsail, since it was clear that his friendly French flag was not inducing the master to slacken pace. It

19

was then he began to regret not having let the gunners have more practice during the week at sea. (Powder and cannon shot were very expensive.) First the balls dropped far short; then they winged into the air and only a distant plopping indicated where they had fallen. Almost at once a gun replied from the other vessel. Stephen recognized it as a French long four-pounder; it could not reach them yet but could do damage at closer quarters. If only his own damned gunners could aim straight. He ran forward and saw to the next discharge himself. He might not be a first-class navigator but he had had some experience with cannon.

The Frenchman's best hope of escape was the weather. There was a handy, steady south-westerly breeze but the rain was thickening into mist, and visibility was closing in. It would be a disaster to lose touch now. Hodge was the only man who could speak fair French so Stephen sent him up into the bows with a hailer, telling them that the *Adolphus* was friendly and saying that his captain wanted to speak with their captain as he had news of Bonaparte.

The only answer to this was a heavy thump in the bows and splinters of wood flying up through the air. Stephen cursed and lowered the sight of his cannon, ordered them to fire. The cannon reared on the deck, two stabs of flame lit the grey afternoon, but the brig had dipped at the wrong moment and both shots ploughed harmlessly into the sea.

Close to, the *Revenant* was quite a handsome vessel, well cared for and every way in good

20

shape. She was sailing heavy and probably carried a full cargo. Of course she would have to be boarded, and that was what the crew was waiting for — eagerly crouching behind the elmwood bulwarks. They looked a villainous lot, and he hoped sight of them swarming up over the side would persuade the Frenchman to strike and thus save damage and bloodshed. The *Revenant* with her equally high bulwarks could prove a nasty customer if defended stoutly.

Jason was beside him. "You're firing too low, Father! What range have those guns? If we could smash their rudder . . . "

"Do not forget we want to *capture* this ship," said Stephen, "not sink her." Another shot whistled over their head and tore a clean hole in their gaff mainsail. The *Adolphus* slewed as the sail split, until Carter at the helm brought her up again. "Now back to your place and no more talking." Stephen was leading one boarding party, Hodge the other. Jason was in Hodge's party. Carter was remaining in charge of the *Adolphus*.

At much closer range now the two six-pounders fired and this time the shot found their mark. The great mainsail, carrying the full thrust of the wind, was suddenly in flapping tatters. The larger balls and the double shot had done far more damage to the Frenchman's sail; the *Revenant* yawed, and the two vessels closed. Muskets began to fire, and some misfired in the damp and the rain. One ship ran alongside the other with a grinding crump, grappling irons were thrown, men were over and jumping down onto the deck. There was some fighting but it was half-hearted. The man at the helm looked like the Captain, and grouped around him were a half-dozen others, cutlasses out, pistols firing. But one man fell and then another and the Captain raised his hands.

Stephen let out a yell of triumph — it had all come just as he had planned it; a splendid prize! But there was another yell close beside him and a rough hand pulled at his shoulder, tugging him round. On the *Revenant*'s larboard bow something else was looming out of the mist. She was far bigger than either of the contestants: two decks, three masts, a rakish bow. There was ice in Stephen's stomach as he recognized the French frigate which had chased them on Friday.

2

IT was luck that they got away at all — the luck being that the *Adolphus* had grappled the *Revenant* on the starboard side, so that the French *chaloupe* was between the *Adolphus* and the frigate and the frigate could not fire at the English ship without hitting the *Revenant*.

A panic retreat for Stephen's men — up and over the side, and back to their brig, hacking at grappling irons that failed to come free, Carter bringing over the helm as the last man dropped aboard; both ships had been travelling at a modest speed when they came alongside; Carter made skilful use of the sail already set, and they had the weather gage. Quite quickly they slipped into the mist as the frigate sent a broadside after them. Some of it landed, and one man, from Truro, was killed, a second lost his leg. Then they were away.

There was still an hour or so's daylight left, and it all depended on whether the mist would clear at the wrong moment. But it stayed, heavy and morose. Stephen wiped the sweat from his brow and looked around. The bitterest disappointment of his life. A prize of real value, virtually surrendered, prospect of a return to England in triumph with a rich reward — and then all to be dashed from his hands. Presumably the frigate had been attracted by the firing. They were damned lucky not to have been captured.

And then Stephen looked around for Jason and found he was not there.

★ ★ ★

"We'll follow them," said Stephen. "No choice."

"I seen 'im with Jago and Edwards. They went forard and got cut off in the strowl. There's the three on 'em missing. They'm prisoners now, I'll lay a crown."

"Follow 'em?" said Carter. "Tes easier said than done in this misty wet. Like as not we'll find the frigate instead."

"It is clearing," said Stephen between his teeth. "Look, the sky's light where the sun's setting. We'll follow. All through the night, if need be."

Rain ran down their faces as they stood by the helm peering into the light fog. A pink haze flushed the mist astern of them; the rain might well lift with the onset of evening. But that was only one of their problems.

"Where are we?" said Stephen.

"Dear knows," said Carter, "unless the stars d'come out. And then twill only be at best guesswork so far as the land d'go. But I've a fancy we're nigh in to the French coast."

"I didn't think so. What makes ye say that?"

"Notice them two French fishing boats coming up as we was going to board the *chaloupe*? They was crabbers. They'd not be far off the coast."

"Near Dinard, d'ye reckon?"

24

"Not so far's that. More like Cap Fréhel."

"The *Revenant* came from St Pierre," said Hodge. "Twas on the tiller."

"Where is St Pierre?"

"Just north of St Malo. I know it well. Upon times when we was running goods to Roscoff we'd come east to St Pierre instead. Twas quieter and prices was better."

Stephen walked up and down, up and down. So far they had been cruising more than a week and now were being sent empty away. And he had lost Jason. To his own surprise this counted for more than anything else.

"Think you could find St Pierre?" he said to Hodge.

"Maybe if the fog d'clear."

"It would depend upon you and Carter," Stephen said. "I've not a great knowledge of this coast, but I know it's rocks. And the tides are lethal. But I've a fancy to follow the *Revenant* in."

Hodge took out his watch. "If we're near Cap Fréhel, as Mike says, we could be off St Pierre by midnight. So long as we don't fall foul of the frigate again we could run in and see how the land lies."

★ ★ ★

At one o'clock in the morning they ran in to see how the land lay.

St Pierre was a fishing village, not unlike its opposite fellows in Cornwall. A horseshoe harbour with stone-built cottages climbing

25

steeply up the granite hillside behind. A harbour wall, a tidal inlet, a church tower showing against the skyline. Even at that time in the morning there were a few lights.

The weather was not unsuitable for a raid. Thick fine rain still borne on a light sou'westerly breeze. The moon had just risen and, though obscured by clouds, prevented the harbour from being altogether dark.

The *Adolphus*, in total darkness, had dropped anchor just inside the harbour wall. They went in in the two jolly boats. Fortunately the sea was light, for each boat was crammed to the gunnels with men. There was hardly room in them to row. Each man carried a cutlass. Stephen had forbidden muskets, even pistols. "They may squirt us," said Stephen. "They won't be able to shoot us tonight."

But apart from the soaking damp, the essence of the adventure was silence.

There were only three ships in the tiny harbour and they could easily pick out the *Revenant* as the largest and because of its unusual trim. Farther up were a dozen rowing boats stranded in the sand. A light in a cottage. A light in the *Revenant*, somewhere below decks. A swinging lantern as someone moved along the quay.

On Stephen's direction they did not come alongside the *chaloupe* but paddled slowly past it, and each boat attached itself to a weed-grown iron ladder going up the harbour wall. One man was left in each boat. Stephen led the rest up to the cobble-stoned quay.

At the top he looked cautiously around, but the swinging lantern had gone. The village appeared to be asleep.

There was still the chink of light from the *Revenant*, and as Stephen dropped gently upon its forepeak he saw that this came from the main cabin. Followed by six other men, including Hodge, he crept along the deck and down the companion way. A light under the cabin door. Stephen drew his cutlass and went in.

It was the captain, sitting before a desk adding up figures in his log book. Beside him was an elderly man in a dark suit, also with a book open in front of him.

The captain half got to his feet before Stephen was across the room with the knife at his throat. Hodge had come up behind the elderly man, who looked like a merchant. The other men crowded into the cabin; the last one quietly shut the door.

"Ask him," said Stephen. "Ask him where he has put his prisoners."

Hodge spoke sharply to the captain, who was trying to focus his eyes on the knife so close to his throat. A second demand brought a sharp response.

Hodge said: "They be locked in a fish cellar at the end o' the quay."

Stephen said: "Tell him he shall lead us there. If he makes a sound I will cut his throat. You, Vage, and you, Moon, stay with this other man. If he utters a word open him up. *Now* . . . "

The captain was forced to his feet and thrust out of the cabin. Stephen whispered orders to his men still clustered on the deck. They were to stay quiet until he called them, remain where their shapes would not be seen. Then he named the three from the cabin, and Hodge, to go with him.

It was a shambling dark procession which made its way to the end of the long quay. The only sound was when someone caught his foot on an uneven flagstone or splashed into a pool of water. Mindful of his own life, the captain was as quiet as anyone. He stopped before a big stone-built shed on the edge of the village. From here you could see the one light, which was in fact several lights when you got closer, and came from the windows of an inn. Talking and laughter could be heard.

The captain stood before the door of the shed and spread his hands helplessly.

"What does he say?" demanded Stephen.

"That he does not have the key to the padlock."

The knife came nearer to the Frenchman's throat. "Where is it?"

"He says the gendarme will have it. He be in Le Lion d'Or."

Stephen stooped to peer at the padlock. He gestured to Hodge to try to force the lock with his cutlass, but it was clear that the knife would break first.

"Reckon we'd best go," one of the men muttered. "They'll come to no 'urt as prisoners . . . "

"Shut your trap!" Stephen snapped. "Keast, go you back to the *chaloupe* and find a marling

28

spike. Hurry, but stay quiet."

"Aye, aye," said Keast and turned and slipped back the way they had come.

Now that there was nothing to do but wait they could take in the noises inside the inn. The sailors had returned safely after a long voyage and were celebrating. Particularly, thought Stephen, they were celebrating the narrow escape they had had this afternoon from capture and a long internment in England.

He bent to the door and listened. He could certainly hear nothing inside, and the monstrous thought came to him that perhaps the French captain was deceiving him. If he was he should pay with his life. Leaving Hodge to guard the captain, he walked round the cellar: there were no windows but there might have been another door. There was, but when he opened it it led into a small room with bags of salt. He came back to the front and stooped by the door again.

"Jason," he called.

No answer.

"Tell him," Stephen said to Hodge, "if the prisoners are not here I will kill him." Hodge was about to speak when Stephen said: "Wait."

There was a burst of laughter from the inn.

"Jason!" he said again.

"Father!" It was a whisper.

Stephen felt a surge of triumph. "Jason. Quiet, boy. We have come to get ye. Are you well?"

"Jago has a bad leg. I am well. And Tom Edwards. Father, can you open the door?"

"Not yet. Have patience. And keep quiet. Can Jago walk?"

There was a murmur inside. "He says he will try."

"He *must* try."

A warning hand touched his arm. The door of the inn opened and two men came out. The lantern light flooded over the cobbled street as they came arm in arm towards the crouching group; then they turned up the quay towards the *Revenant*.

They were both well gone in drink and stumbled several times on the way, supporting each other.

They were half-way up the quay when little Keast slid out of the gloom beside the waiting men, who had been so concerned to watch the French sailors that they had not seen him coming back. He carried two marling spikes. "Reckoned one might break," he said.

Stephen attacked the lock with less regard to silence than he had previously shown. There should be plenty of his men waiting to receive the two Frenchmen when they stepped aboard, but whether they could be disposed of without rousing the town remained to be seen.

The first spike bent but the second, forced in on top of it, did the trick. The padlock broke. The door squeaked open. Jason came out first, flung his arms round his father.

"Didn't I say, lads? Didn't I say he'd come for us?"

"Quiet!" said Stephen, giving his son a hug. "And quick. Now come on, quick. There's much still to do. But *quiet*, everybody!"

Two of the other men were helping Jago out. Edwards too was limping. In all this the thoughtful Hodge was still holding a knife to the captain's throat.

There was still no sound from the *Revenant*, so it looked as if the returning sailors had been taken care of.

The party began to return along the quay. The rain was heavier than ever, misting men only a few yards from each other.

They reached the *Revenant*. Twelve men shinned down the ladder to return to the jolly boats, cast off, pulled round to the stern of the *chaloupe*; four other men ran the length of the ship, dropped lines to the boats, which began to row away. Hodge had gone below with the captain. Jago and Edwards were aboard. Keast and another man had cast off the stern rope securing the *Revenant* to a bollard. Stephen and Jason stooped to throw off the forward rope.

"Halt!" shouted a voice. "*Nom de la République! Qui va là?*"

It was a French soldier who had come suddenly out of the moonlit fog. For a second they stared at each other. Stephen lifted his cutlass. The soldier discharged his musket full in Stephen's face.

The hammer came down to strike the cap and the cap failed to detonate.

Stephen laughed out loud and stabbed the man in the chest. Then, unable to withdraw his cutlass, he left it in the fallen figure and jumped aboard the *Revenant* as Jason cast off.

The two boats began to row the *chaloupe* out of the harbour, and the Cornishmen swarmed up the rigging preparing to make sail.

3

IF anyone had spoken of 'the dark night of the soul' to Demelza she would not have known where the words came from but she would perfectly have understood what they meant.

When Julia died all those years ago it had been when she was just recovering from the morbid sore throat herself and she had felt the loss as a mortal blow from which she could hardly recover. Julia had been nineteen months old. But she and Ross were young, and after all the despair, which had included Ross's trial for his life and near bankruptcy, they had somehow climbed together out of a pit, which had never seemed so deep since.

But Jeremy, their second child, was twenty-four. Born in a time of great stress, he had been with them ever since, through all the vicissitudes of life, all their joys, all their sorrows. Because of that, because of his age, he was more a part of the family than any of the three younger ones — even Clowance, who was only three years younger. What she had said to Caroline was only the truth: whenever she thought of Jeremy she thought of a thousand days of caring.

When she last saw him, last December, he had grown better looking. The tall loose-jointed young man with a tendency to stoop had filled out with his army training, had matured, his hair long, his face less clear-skinned, his smile more sophisticated. No wonder Cuby had at last fallen in love with him.

Too late to save him from the army, a captaincy, and a march to his death in the mud of Flanders. Demelza knew that Clowance blamed Cuby for this, saying it was his broken love-affair that had spurred him to go into the army. It could be true; Demelza was not sure; there was another reason which perhaps only she would ever know. Though there were a man and a woman somewhere, one of them probably her son-in-law, who might yet throw light on the subject. (Not that she wanted light. Better for it always to be hidden, as the sacks had been hidden, in the dark cave in Kellow's Ladder.)

Last time he was home he had seemed on the point of saying something to her, attempting an explanation of the unexplainable. "Perhaps in joining the army I was trying to escape from myself." And then, when he had seen the loving cup, which she had carefully cleaned and polished and put on the sideboard, he had said: "Someday, sometime — not now — perhaps when we are both a few years older — I would like to talk to you."

And she had smiled at him and said: "Don't leave it too late."

It had been prophetic without her knowing it. With the war over it had then been much more likely that she would predecease him. She only wished it had been so.

On Sunday, the 16th July Demelza for once was on her own. Nothing seemed to get better with the passage of the days. This morning she had walked only as far along the beach as Wheal Leisure and then turned back, having neither the energy nor the initiative to go further. A rarely beautiful day, the night wind having dropped as the sun came up, the whole beach in a state of warm confusion as the waves trembled and broke and piled up and trembled and broke again, a magisterial demonstration of power and authority. These were neap-tides, so there was not so much of a run as sometimes, but every now and then a feathery froth of water an inch or two deep slithered up to and around her feet, soaking her shoes and the hem of her skirt.

She might as well go in, she thought, and make a dish of tea; though she was neither thirsty nor hungry. It was something to do.

John Gimlett stood in front of her. She looked up at this unexpected sight.

"The master is back."

"*What? When?*"

"'Alf an hour gone. Didn't know quite where to find ee, ma'am."

Demelza hastened her step, but not too much. She did not feel quite able to face him.

He was in the garden, her garden, looking at some of her flowers. At first she hardly recognized him, he looked so very old.

She came to the gate, opened it. He heard the click of the latch, looked up.

"Ross!" She flew to him.

Gimlett discreetly went in by the yard door.

★ ★ ★

35

"Take more tea," she said. "You must be thirsty after so long a ride."

"Your garden," he said. "It has lacked your touch."

"Like other things," she said. "But twill alter now."

"Your hollyhocks . . . "

"Jane said they was damaged by a late frost. And I think your mother's lilac tree needs hard cutting, else it will die."

"Had you just been to the mine?"

"No, no. I was walking . . . Ben has been very good. Everyone has been very good. You're so *thin*, Ross."

A cow was roaring somewhere in the valley. It was a distant, rural sound, almost lost in the silence of the house.

"There's so much to tell you," Ross said, "I don't know where to begin."

"Maybe the first day you are home is not the right time."

"I lay at Tregothnan last night," he said. "I put in at St Austell, thought I could reach home, borrowed a nag but the nag went lame . . . If there is one recurring theme in my history it is that every horse I hire or borrow goes lame . . . Or is shot from under me — "

"One was shot from under you?"

"Two, to be exact. But that is for telling some other time. Demelza."

"Yes?"

"Can you believe it is only in January that we left here? It has been a lifetime."

"More than a lifetime."

"Aye, that too."

She busied herself, pouring more tea for him and then for herself. They both took milk but no sugar. Tea with sugar is not a Cornish custom.

"Little Jane Ellery was bit by a dog yesterday," she said. "A stray dog near Sawle. He behaved very strange and snatched and snarled, so I think they have put him down. They called Dwight and to be safe he cut into the tooth marks to make a clean wound and then disinfected it with nitric acid. Poor little Jane squealed her head off, but a sweetmeat seemed soon to set her to rights. But of course they will be anxious for a day or two."

Ross sipped his tea. They sat quietly in the parlour.

Demelza said: "On Friday Sephus Billing killed an adder with five young in it. He was drawing potatoes at the time. Side of the Long Field."

"They were always fond of that wall," Ross said. "My father often warned me."

"Jud used to call them long cripples," Demelza said.

"I know."

The brightness of the day outside made the parlour dark.

Demelza said: "And how is Cuby?"

"She will come later. I told her she must stay with us until after the baby is born. Then she must decide her own life. You would agree with that?"

"Yes. Oh, yes."

Ross said: "She was very good most of the time. She only broke down once. I have never heard a woman sob like it. It was — such an ugly noise — like someone sawing wood."

"Don't."

Ross said: "I was so fortunate just to find Jeremy in time. He did not seem to be in any pain. He — he sent his love to you and asked us to look after Cuby."

Demelza got up, took out a handkerchief and gently dabbed his eyes. Then she wiped her own.

"There is much to do here, Ross. We have been neglecting our home. Some of the seed is not sown yet. And we need to sell some lambs — I waited for you to know how many. And the damp in the library ceiling is getting worse."

He looked at her.

She said: "And there's the white store turnips. Cal Trevail was asking me yesterday — "

"Why are you alone like this? I thought you would never be left alone."

"They did their best . . . Stephen came back from some successful adventure last week. When he heard about Jeremy he came straight over, stayed two nights. He had to go back, then, but wanted Clowance to stay on. I said *no*. I said *no*, you would be here soon, and for a little while I *wanted* to be alone. Twas true. I had no talk left. My tongue has been heavy all the time — ever since I knew."

"But the others. Verity and — "

"Verity left on Tuesday because Andrew is very slight. It is some heart affection. Caroline's two girls are just home and she has not seen them for a term. Henry is in the cove with Mrs Kemp and they should be back soon. Isabella-Rose is at school."

"You sent her?"

"To Mrs Hemple's for half a term. I sent her before I — had your letter."

"How did she take the news?"

"As you would expect," said Demelza lightly, controlling herself. "The piano needs tuning badly. The damp air gets at the strings. And this old spinet, do you think we should throw it out, Ross?"

"Never. It is too much a part of our lives . . . The Falmouths sent their love and sympathy."

"Good of them. I expect they will be concerned about Fitzroy. Many, many people have sent their love and sympathy, Ross. Tis very — warming to have so much — love and sympathy. Even Mr Odgers . . . I think we shall have to do something about Mr Odgers soon, Ross. He took off his wig in church last Sunday, I'm told, and threw it at the choir. He said afterwards he thought he was driving away the greenfly. They have been very bad this year, the greenfly; I think it is the warm summer."

Ross said: "And how is Clowance?"

"Well. But you know how she felt for Jeremy."

"And Stephen?"

Demelza put her tea-cup back on the tray and got up.

"Will you take me for a bathe, Ross?"

"What?" He stared again.

"The sea is heavy, so heavy and the sun is broiling. I have not bathed since last year — I could not without you."

Ross hesitated. "It is not seemly on my first day home."

"Nor is it," said Demelza, "but I want you to do it for me — with me. There is time before dinner. It will help — I think it will help — to wash away our tears."

* * *

Ross said: "I am worried about Demelza."

"Yes," said Dwight, then nodded his head. "Yes."

"She is physically well, so far as you know?"

"She has made no complaints. Of course the shock is still affecting her."

"Yet not in some ways quite as I would have expected. I am happy if it is sincere but — well, she is so full of interest in all the affairs of Nampara — just as if nothing had happened."

"Is that how she seems to you? It is not as she has been before you came. She cared for nothing. Often she would not talk even to her family. She spoke to Caroline, but very little. Most times she would just sit there."

"You think, then, this show of liveliness has been put on for my benefit?"

"She's a very strong personality, Ross. She may feel that she has to be supportive of you."

"If it is put on, one wonders how long it will endure — and can only guess at what it is hiding."

40

"It may not change. Once you have assumed a mantle it may become a part of everyday wear."

Ross had ridden over and found Dwight in his laboratory, Caroline and the children being out riding. Dwight had walked out with him and they were sitting on a wooden garden seat looking across the lawn towards some trees, beyond which, if you walked a little farther, you could see Sawle Church.

"It is difficult to tell her anything about what happened," Ross said. "She heads me off, turns the point, brings up some other subject. Well, perhaps that is natural. One cannot go on probing at a wound — or should not, I imagine. Last night . . . "

He stopped. Dwight said nothing, staring at a squirrel swarming up the branch of a tree.

"Last night," Ross said, "she would hardly let me touch her. We lay beside each other in bed, just holding hands. When I woke early this morning just as it was coming light she was gone, standing by the window looking out. When she heard me move she came back, slipped into bed, took my hand again."

Dwight said: "When Caroline lost Sarah . . . You remember? She left me, went to London, stayed with her aunt. I did not know when, or if, she was coming back. This is much, much worse — for Demelza *and* for you. Sarah was a baby — like your Julia. Jeremy was just happily married, everything before him. I can only guess at what you both feel."

The squirrel had disappeared. Rooks were

clapping their wings somewhere. They sounded like an unenthusiastic audience.

Ross said: "Of course there is much I cannot tell her — would not. You saw my letter to her?"

"Yes."

"I said little enough about that last day ... When Wellington entrusted me with the message for Prince Frederick of the Netherlands I knew the distance to be about ten miles, but I expected to be back in the very early afternoon. But on the way back — perhaps I was a thought incautious and steered too close to the fighting — I was almost overrun by a French cavalry charge. Then my horse was killed, and as I fell with it a piece of round shot struck me in the chest — just below the chest — and I was knocked out for what must have been half an hour. And for a time after that I could barely stand."

Ross fumbled in his pocket and took out a piece of crumpled metal which Dwight could see had been a watch.

"My father's," said Ross. "It was the one thing the French left me when I was interned. When I escaped I intended to sell it to buy food or shelter or perhaps a weapon of some sort; but in the end I did not have to. Had I done so I should not be here today."

Dwight took the crushed watch, turned it over. The face had gone altogether, and the gold case was splayed as if it had been hit with a hammer.

"Then that is one piece of extraordinary good fortune."

"It was intended for Jeremy. If I had given it him perhaps he would be here instead of me. Better if it had been that way."

"Have you shown this to Demelza?"

"No. Nor shall do."

"Well . . . perhaps not. Not yet anyway."

The sun came out, warming them as they sat together, two old friends.

"There are many things I cannot tell her," Ross said, "even if she would listen. That night after Jeremy's death I could not sleep. I was not hungry but was sickly empty of stomach — and thirsty, so thirsty — and black with powder and stiff from my small injuries. I lay down in the hut for a while, trying to wrap an old blanket round me — just beside him — but after a while I got up again and began to wander about the battlefield. There were many still wounded, crying for attention, but I was too dazed to help — and in any case had no means to help — no salves, no bandages, no water. Have you ever seen a battlefield, Dwight?"

"No."

"I had. Or thought I had. Not like this. Never anything like this. Of course you have been in a battle at sea, have suffered the horrors of the prisoner-of-war camp . . . "

"Yes . . . "

"Before he died Jeremy spoke of the horses. They were almost the worst part of it. Some were lying with their entrails hanging out, yet still alive. Others dragged themselves around in terrible stages of mutilation. Some were simply wandering loose, having lost their owners. I caught one such and rode as far south as Quatre Bras, where all the fighting had been on the Friday."

"Was the fighting at Waterloo over by this time?"

"Almost. There were some Prussian troops still about, and not too particular whom they shot at; there were a few camps of them, bivouacking, cooking their meals; but the main body had passed on. Quatre Bras was a ghastly sight. You of all people must be familiar with what happens to a body after it is dead."

"Yes . . ."

"Those at Quatre Bras had mostly been dead for two days. It was a brilliant moonlit night, with only a rare cloud passing across the moon. In the moonlight they looked like negroes."

"Yes . . ."

"And swollen into grotesque shapes. Bursting out of their uniforms — those who were left with uniforms. Many had been stripped naked by the peasants; most of those who had not, lay upon their faces with their pockets pulled out and their boots taken, their papers scattered everywhere. Of course it was not just the peasants. The soldiers themselves: the French when they advanced, the British and Germans when the French retreated . . . The stench in the courtyard of the farm at Quatre Bras was intolerable . . . Perhaps you wonder why I tell you all this."

"No, I think it should be spoken of."

"There is no one else I would say this to. When I was in America as a young man I saw

44

enough to fill my crop. But not like this. That was skirmishing. This was head-on conflict of a most terrible kind."

They sat for a while in silence. Ross fingered his scar.

"I found one man still alive. That is why I went into the yard of the farmhouse; there's a well there; I went to get him water. Why he was alive I don't know; his skull was crushed; but some people take a deal of killing. He was a Frenchman, and when he found I understood him he asked me to kill him and finish off his misery."

Dwight glanced at Ross's lean, restless face. More than ever lean now, and the veins in his neck showing.

"I found I could not, Dwight. There had been so much blood spilt; for three days I had been surrounded by death. And then I thought of the French brigadier, whom I had come greatly to like and respect, even though he was a Bonapartist. And I knew he would say it was only a kindness to kill this suffering man. Perhaps even a duty. But still I could not."

"I think you were right."

"I spent more time on him than anyone else on the battlefield. I bathed his face and his crushed head and tried to tie up his other wounds. Then I put a beaker of water beside him and left him — presumably to die."

"Were there no surgeons anywhere?"

"A few. Working desperately, trying to help the worst wounded. Though from the way I saw them treating men then and afterwards in

Brussels, I wonder if they did not help to kill off more wounded men than they cured."

"Ours is still a primitive science."

Ross got up. "By God, I should think so! But you, Dwight, have often said that your profession was over-fond of the leech. You bleed your patients far less than most of your fellows. These men — these so-called surgeons — were bleeding men who had lost half their blood already!"

Dwight got up too, patted his leg with the little riding cane he carried. "The medical view is that if a wound is inflamed, bleeding will help to reduce the inflammation. It's not a theory I totally subscribe to — as you know — but I was not there and so cannot speak much against them. I'm afraid most physical treatment is rough and ready. Not least when it comes to war."

"The arms and legs that were hacked off! I know it is better than gangrene — we both know too well that — that anything is better than gangrene . . . But afterwards, to sterilize with hot tar, and then, as like as not, a clyster of soap and water and a pill of senna pods in lard, to clear the humours!"

They began to walk across the paddock towards the distant trees.

After a minute Dwight said: "Is your ankle . . . ?"

"Well enough."

They walked on.

"Where is Demelza now?"

"I left her in the garden with Matthew Mark

46

Martin. Jane Gimlett says she has hardly been in it since she came home."

"We have never spoken of your baronetcy. I believe it was a good thing to take."

"Good? Dear God! It is a cynical twist that Jeremy will now no longer be here to inherit it."

"Henry will."

Ross looked up. "Maybe. Well, yes. If *he* survives."

"There should be no wars after this for generations. And if there were Henry would have no need to take part. You have three handsome children left."

"And a grandchild on the way . . . It was strange how I met Cuby. And horrible. On the Monday morning I was able to purloin a farm cart and I put my horse — the one I had found on Sunday night — into the shafts, and I lifted — I lifted my son into the back and covered him with a blanket. The road back to Brussels was — impossible, with the sick and wounded, with returning soldiers, with ambulances and wagons; but we went with the stream. Then I saw this coach coming *against* the stream with a man riding before it with a drawn sword, forcing people to give way. I paid them little attention, for I was too sunk in my own sorrow. But I remember noticing that the coach horses were screaming with fright. Coming into the battle zone from Brussels, they were not used to the smell of blood and corruption. Then suddenly a voice called: 'Captain Poldark!' It was Cuby, my daughter-in-law."

They stopped at the edge of the paddock. The vegetation here was lush with cow parsley and ragged robin and wild marguerites. Ross wiped his forehead.

"In all those days of battle that was the second worst moment for me. Her round pretty anxious face changed when I told her, she went deathly pale. She jumped down and insisted — *insisted* on seeing Jeremy, on uncovering his face . . . Then — then she looked at me as if I had stabbed her to the heart. Which indeed I had — and would have given my own life willingly not to have done so."

Bees were humming around a clump of foxgloves, struggling in and out of the bells like fat robbers peering into caves.

Ross said: "Sir William de Lancey, Wellington's Chief of Staff, had been gravely wounded, and his wife was forcing her way out to Waterloo to see him. Cuby had asked if she might have a lift and had been given one . . . There were other women going out, amid all the confusion, seeking their husbands, hoping to find them alive. Magdalene de Lancey found her husband and nursed him for a week in a cottage in Waterloo, and then he died."

They began to walk back.

Dwight said: "It is hot today. Let's go indoors for a while. Will you take a glass of lemonade?"

Ross gave a short harsh laugh. "In most of the crises of my life, the big disappointments — as when Elizabeth married Francis — the tragedy when we lost Julia — the stresses when Demelza became infatuated with Hugh Armitage — and they all seem to be *dwarfed* — *are* dwarfed — by this; in all of them I have taken to the brandy bottle. Now I am offered lemonade!"

"There is brandy if you want it."

"I drank very little after Jeremy's death; first because there was *nothing* — except one flask I found half full of *genever*. Then I was preoccupied looking after Cuby. Then there were the burial arrangements. With one thing and another . . . I drank more than usual on the trip home, but the taste was lacking. As my medical man, would you advise a glass of lemonade at this stage?"

"I am going to take one."

"It guarantees absolute oblivion?"

"As good as brandy in the long run."

Ross said: "I'm not sure that I want to regard anything in the long run from now on . . . Tell me, Dwight, one thing extra that has been concerning me . . . "

"Yes?"

"You know Demelza all her life has been a thought fond of drink — some drink — chiefly port. When I returned yesterday there was no sign. Have you seen any sign?"

"I have hardly seen her in the evening, but Caroline would have mentioned it, I am sure."

"She did over-drink at one time, you know. I came home one night and found her incapable. That was about a year ago."

"I didn't know. I'm sorry."

"It never happened again. Perhaps it was a passing phase. Human nature is unfathomable, is it not? Demelza has lost her dearly beloved son and yet appears to stay sober. I am in similar straits and content myself with lemonade. Perhaps grief — real grief — brings sobriety. Or are we just growing old and no longer consider it worth while to make gestures of protest?"

"I suspect you will live to make many more gestures of protest yet," said Dwight, "but they are no better for being seen through the bottom of a brandy glass."

4

STEPHEN said: "It has been a bitter time for you, dear heart; and in truth tis sad for me. All I said to your mother was God's truth. Jeremy was a real true friend. We did — many things together. All through the time when you and I were estranged, him and me, we were still friends. In that year when we was separated he never, of course, took my side against you, but he was never anything but sympathetic to the way I felt. In fact we were both deprived in a similar way. It made for a fellow feeling. He was a brave man and it's bitter, bitter that he should be gone now, just when he was happy married and his wife expecting a baby. An' I'm deeply sorry."

"Thank you, Stephen."

He was rowing her back from the *Adolphus*, which she had been visiting for the first time since its famous voyage.

"And thank you for this lovely present," she added, fingering the heavy coral necklace about her throat. "It is marvellous pretty, and I want to wear it all the time."

"So you shall. And others I shall buy you."

He paused in his rowing, allowed the boat to drift of its own momentum.

"Jeremy's death," he said, "Jeremy's death has put a damper on what I did; but I can't but rejoice at the way everything else has turned up

51

aces for me — for the both of us. I can't but rejoice, Clowance, and that's God's truth too."

"I don't expect you to. In a month — in a few months — I expect I shall be able to rejoice with you."

"Ye must be able to rejoice now, that we are right out of the wood!"

"Are we *really* safe?"

"Oh yes. Oh yes. By a long haul."

"Can you bear to tell me again?" Clowance asked, knowing that he would like nothing better. "At Nampara, in the bedroom, it seemed so unreal beside Jeremy's death, I could hardly take it in. You captured this ship called — called . . . "

"*Revenant.* She was a *chalouper.* What in England we more or less call a sloop. But bigger than we build 'em in England. She was bigger than we were, bigger than a packet ship, and carried a crew, I reckon, of about twenty-five, and four four-pounders and any amount of small arms. *And* when we rescued Jason and the other two, we bore away with us the captain and a rich merchant who were aboard at the time, and can be ransomed!"

"Why did you take the — the *chaloupe* to Bristol?"

"I knew more people there, see. And to tell the truth I was wary of Sir George. Ye know, the Warleggans have a long reach, and after what has happened I wouldn't trust him as far as I can spit. I thought, maybe somehow he'll try to seize part of the cargo in lieu of a debt — or say it was illegal because of the end of the war and should be returned — or any trumped up charge. I thought I was safer in Bristol. I thought first of Plymouth, but I felt safer going home."

Clowance shivered slightly; she could not have told why, for the day was warm.

Stephen did not notice. "Mind, there was a time when I regretted that choosing. Once safe across the Channel, I crept close in to the English coast, not fancying a meeting with a French frigate again; but not far off Penzance the weather turned foul; a strong gale blew up sudden from the south. There was a great peril of being embayed, so I set every stitch of canvas the masts would bear and began to claw off the shore. The *Revenant* was hull down way to the south-east of us and riding it out well. I've never seen *Adolphus* in such a state before. She plunged through the water so fast clouds of spray were frothing to her very topsails. I thought the canvas would any minute carry away. But it did not, and after an hour the worst was over. Both vessels rounded Land's End before nightfall."

Clowance let her hand trail in the water. "And the cargo?"

"M' dear, we're rich! Not rich by Warleggan standards, but well found and independent of Warleggans for good an' all. *Revenant* was eighteen days out of New York. Skins, all sorts of skins to make coats; leather and boots; saddlery; 50 tons of pig iron, steel rods, five cases of apothecaries' wares, 36 wheels and axles, 48 kettles — I lost count . . . Aside from the value of the ship itself!"

"And what is happening now?"

"The Cornish Naval Bank has a corresponding partner, as they call it, in Bristol. As the money comes in, twill be transferred into my name in Falmouth. I was tempted to stay on and on, but I felt I must come back and see you, tell you this wonderful news. Alas, that you had such bad news yourself!"

"You have shareholders to pay?"

"Oh, yes. And the crew. But the crew I have now paid off. They're all roaring happy and consider themselves rich, small though their portions are compared to mine." Stephen shipped one oar and steered past some wreckage floating in the harbour. "The shareholders will take thirty-five per cent. The rest will set us up very nicely, and *very* independent."

"Have you seen Warleggan's Bank yet?"

"No. I shall go in tomorrow. All the way home — and twas none too placid a trip for July neither — I have been asking myself how I ought to do it. I thought at first just to tell them straight just what I thought of 'em. I thought over just what I should say. But then I considered further and changed me mind. I've decided to act just as he might act if he was in my shoes."

"What does that mean, Stephen?"

"I shall act very polite. I shall tell 'em nothing of what I have been doing or what profits I have made — though no doubt they'll hear about it or already have. I shall go in tomorrow and see Lander and simply say: 'Good-day to ye, Mr Lander, it so happens that I have been able to obtain finance through another bank, and as they impose no restrictions, well, I think I shall transfer my account to them from the end of this week. Any accommodation bills I have signed, Mr Lander, will be paid the moment they come due, and I will continue, with your permission, Mr Lander, to trade in Penryn and Falmouth as an independent shipper.' Something like that, but smoother. 'Good-day to ye, Mr Lander,'I shall say. 'I hope I find you well. Now it so happens, quite by chance, like, that I have been approached by another bank, who offer me all the accommodation I need without imposing any restrictions as to the overdraft I choose to carry — '"

"I am glad you will do it that way because — "

"Well, because of Harriet, in the main, who helped me survive. And also — well, look you, we might still go to Cardew sometime. I reckon if George can go in for being a hypocrite, so can I!"

Coming in towards the quay, they had to row between a couple of rotting hulks long since grounded in the mud. It was half tide and the barnacled ribs stuck up into the warm sunlight, glinting green and black and orange.

"And from now it will be legitimate trading again?"

"Oh yes. No choice anyhow. The war is over. It all just worked in time for us."

"For us, yes."

This time he did notice her shiver. "Sorry, sorry, it will be a sore place for a long while."

After a minute she said: "And Jason?"

"Jason?"

"He will — stay on with you?"

"For sure . . . " He allowed the slight current to carry them in.

"D'ye know, it was the greatest moment when I broke into the fish cellar and rescued him. I think then I really came up to his expectations of me as a father! . . . And then to steal away with the *Revenant* right from under their noses! It was Nelson stuff! D'ye know, I've got me quite a reputation, Clowance."

"Yes?" She smiled at him.

"Yes. When I took me prize into Bristol — that was a brave moment too! We worked into the harbour no more than five minutes ahead of *Revenant*, which, as is the custom, was flying the British flag atop the French flag flown upside down. Lord, when we got to the quay there was a crowd cheering! And the crews cheered too, you stake your life, knowing the pickings that were going to be theirs! . . . And though I took me prize to Bristol all those sailors were Cornishmen, from Penryn and Falmouth mainly, and they haven't been slow to tell folk of the success of the voyage and the way we took out the Frenchman. Why, if I asked for another crew today I should be swamped wi' volunteers!"

The dinghy slid slowly in beside the quay. Stephen hooked the painter over a bollard and jumped out to give Clowance a hand.

"We'll get the house being built again right away. And this time I shall buy meself a good hunter, as good as Nero. We'll have the stables built first so that they'll be well housed . . . Then we'll ride and hunt together on equal terms!"

"Even when the hunt meets at Cardew?"

"Even then. That's what I said. Another good reason not to fall out with Harriet!" He laughed infectiously and they began to walk up to their cottage hand in hand.

Just below them a half-dozen naked urchins were taking it in turns to leap into the harbour, holding their noses as they jumped and squealing with delight when they came to the surface among the floating seaweed and the apple cores and the driftwood.

"And I have a mind too," he said, "to buy me another ship when the right one comes along at the right price. Three's the proper number, increases the profit, not too many to look after."

"Andrew will be back from New York any time now," said Clowance. "But if this voyage has been a success I do not suppose he will want to leave the Packet Service again."

"I was not thinking of Andrew," Stephen said. "I was thinking of Jason."

When she looked surprised he added: "Oh, I know he is young yet. And he must learn more navigation. I can tell you I'm none too clear on some points meself, but he knows *nothing*. Yet in a year or two he'll be ready for his own ship. Nothing so big as *Adolphus* but maybe the size of the *Lady Clowance*. There was good men on this trip, dear heart, that I'd not employed before. Carter handled the ship real well and Hodge was a godsend. Hodge I must keep in with. Both of 'em I've given special bonuses to. If I buy another vessel one or both of 'em would be ideal to be with Jason on his first voyages, to keep him on course, so to say."

At the entrance to their house she paused, took off her straw hat and let the sunlight and the breezes play with her blonde hair. He looked at her appreciatively. Pity about Jeremy, of course, but you couldn't grieve for ever, and here he was, with a small fortune in the bank — the reward of a daring and dangerous exploit — and with a very peach of a wife who, by her independence and intelligence and refusal to conform to an accepted pattern, intrigued him the more. He wanted her and knew she wanted him. Life was wonderful and he felt wonderful. No one could blame him for that.

The harbour below them was glimmering, iridescent in the sunshine. Beyond it the bay of the Fal, surrounded by cornfields, looked like a majestic garden. Tall masts swung at anchor; towards Trefusis Point a four-masted full-rigged ship was just shaking out her sails. She fired her signal gun to show she was leaving. Small boats were everywhere. People sat on the wall higher up, gossiping in the summer sun.

"I must go to Flushing first thing tomorrow," said Clowance. "Mother tells me Uncle Andrew is serious ill."

"I'll row you," said Stephen, happily conscious that for him all the pressure was off.

★ ★ ★

Andrew Blamey senior had had some sort of a heart seizure, with a fast heart-beat and respiratory trouble. He was sixty-seven, and the apothecary took a grave view of the matter. However, a second man, a physician called Mather, recently arrived from Bath, prescribed Dr Withering's new drug digitalis, with mercury pills, and this produced such a remarkable improvement that when Clowance and Stephen went to see the invalid he was downstairs in his favourite chair by the window watching the movements of shipping through his spyglass.

Stephen was a rare visitor in this house, but was now much more welcome, its being known that, although he had aided young Andrew to leave the Packet Service and embark on some far from respectable adventures, he had now contrived to help Andrew return to the Service with no apparent loss of seniority. Stephen too was very much on his best behaviour today, deferring to Captain Blamey in sea-going matters and answering modestly when Verity questioned him about his exploits. Looking at her second cousin — whom she always regarded as an aunt — Clowance remembered something her father had once said: "Verity was never good-looking but she has the prettiest mouth in Great Britain." Clowance had also heard garbled accounts of how her own mother, defying Poldark hostility to the match, had contrived to bring Captain Blamey and Miss Verity together.

Anyway, it had been a famous match, and it was only a pity that their one child, thoroughly taking and agreeable though he was, could not quite overcome his weakness for gambling and drink.

Clowance was proud of Stephen today. When he set out to subdue his animal spirits and to attune himself to the people he was visiting it was hard to fault his manners or his behaviour. She was grateful to him. It just showed what success could do.

★ ★ ★

Someone of about Blamey's age on the north coast also happened to be ill at this time, but in spite of having the attention of the best physician in the West Country, he refused wilfully to get better. Old Tholly Tregirls, one-armed reprobate and adventurer, having suffered fiercely from asthma all his life, was now dying of something quite different. Ross had just time to call and see him. Tholly died, as he had lived for the last twenty years, at Sally Chill-Offs. When Ross called he raised himself from his bed and said: "Well, Young Cap'n, I hear tell as you've had some ill-luck yourself, eh? Sapling cut off in its prime, eh? Master Jeremy gone. Poor jawb. I reckon twas very poor jawb."

Ross noticed that so far people in the neighbourhood had not changed their form of address to him. He was still 'Cap'n P'ldark', or just 'Cap'n'. That at least was a blessing. But after Tholly had gone there would be no one left to call him 'Young Cap'n' to distinguish him from his father.

"Tis all these 'ere wars," said Tholly, rubbing his scarred and wasted face with a dirty hand. "Public wars, I call 'em. Reckon you was lucky ever to come safe 'ome from that one in 'Merica. Public wars is no good. Public wars don't bring no good to no one. Small wars, private wars, they're different, can profit you upon times."

"Like privateering," said Ross, "or ditching a Preventive man."

Tholly showed his black and broken teeth in a grimace. "That's correct, Young Cap'n, that correct. You know this surgeon — him we rescued from the prison camp all them years agone; that were a great adventure, that were — you'd think he'd do better for me than 'e 'as — out of *gratitude*. Gratitude, you'd think. But he don't put me on me feet. D'ye know after all these years me asthma have *gone*. Cough too. Couldn't cough now if I wished for it. Gone these last six weeks or more. But I can't *eat*. Can't seem t'eat. Sally bring up good soup. But it don't lie."

Ross stared round the small untidy room. Tholly followed his glance.

"I took it off, see? Twas irksome." He waved the stub of his arm towards where the hook and its sheath and leather straps stood upon an old chest of drawers pointing menacingly towards the blackened rafters. "When I'm gone, Young Cap'n, I want you t'ave it, see? Remind you o' me, see. Maybe missus won't like it so well, but put it in your own room, somewhere where she don't go."

Ross went to the open window, where the air

was sweeter. "Thank you, Tholly." He could say nothing else.

Silence fell. Ross thought of Jeremy.

Tholly said: "Reckon I'll never sell you another 'orse."

"Oh maybe, maybe. While there's life."

"I got a long memory for these parts, Young Cap'n. I were born at St Ann's. I mind the time afore ever your 'ouse, afore Nampara was ever builded. Used to be a little pond there, I recollect. There was ducks in it, kept by an old man living in Mellin cottages. Sometimes when twas dry weather, folks in Carnmore — afore Surgeon Choake's time — would send their men with their two cows to drink."

"Ah," said Ross. "How old are you, Tholly?"

"God knows. Or maybe He's forgot too. I mind the two brothers at Trenwith, Charles and Joshua, your papa. Charles were always jealous o' his younger brother. Charles might be comin' in for the big 'ouse and the property, but Joshua were the good-looking one, all the women was attracted to him; then 'e wed the prettiest girl and he came 'ere to live's own carefree life regardless of the county. I remember Joshua building Nampara. Up it went, block by block."

"What year was that, Tholly?"

"God knows . . . I were about eleven year old. Ten or eleven. Miners builded it mostly, Young Cap'n, them as worked at Wheal Grace and all around. That's why tis crude built — not like Trenwith. Reckon Charles's great-great-grandfather had proper masons, brought from up-country. Old Cap'n never cared. I mind he said to me once: 'The longer I live, Tholly, but more God-cursed certain sure I am that the Wise Men never came from the East!' Made me laff, that. He just wanted a place of his own, see? Built near the cove, convenient for him to fish or smuggle, overlooking the beach where he could line-fish and bathe and walk and gallop on the sands. 'E began a line you've kept up, Young Cap'n. Master Jeremy should've stayed home, kept his house. But he didn't, did 'e. More's the pity . . . Well, mebbe the little tacker will — what's his name? — Henry — twill be a pity if the house don't go on, if it all fall to ruin. Old Cap'n started something you shouldn't neglect. Why, who'd be a king in London if he could be a squire in Cornwall?"

It was late afternoon and Ross could see a few people, mainly ragged village folk making their way towards the inn. Sally was a big-bosomed, generous, now elderly woman who had earned her nickname by being willing to let her customers have a little something on credit. 'Just to take the chill off.' They paid her back when they could, most often after a successful 'run'. Tholly had scraped a living as a horse coper and general picker-up of unconsidered trifles and had lived with Sally Tregothnan — some said sponged on her — ever since he returned from the sea. It seemed, if Dwight were correct, that his tenure was coming to an end.

Tholly coughed, but compared to the old days it was a mere genteel clearing of the throat. "I mind them old times well," he said. "Mebbe I

63

remember your mother better than what you do,
Young Cap'n. How old was you when she went
around land? Nine? Ten? . . . She didn't take
to me, thought I were a bad influence. That's
a laff. Whoever thought of influencing the Old
Cap'n? He went his way . . . Mind, he took
heed of she. Good-looking wench. Handsome
handsome long black hair. Upon times I seen
her brushing it when I weren't supposed to. She
'ad a fine temper. It'd flash out like a sword
out of a sheath, silver and sharp and glistening
— cut anyone down. O' course it was agin his
nature."

"What was?"

"Being like 'e was when he was wed to she. It
never come natural to him to toe the line. It was
always 'is way to break the laws, break the rules,
break the standards, see. And 'e carried it off in
such a style — laughing and joking and devil
take it — few folk cared. He was some caution,
was Old Cap'n. Yet for twelve year — twelve
year, mark ee, I never seen 'im chase another
woman. Course he did other things — running
goods, sailing 'ere and there on this and that,
wrecking if the chance came his way, feuding
with landlords and gaugers. But for twelve year
she kept 'im faithful."

"Maybe he wanted to be."

"Oh, stand on that, 'e wanted to be, else
'e wouldn't 've been! My grandfather's ghost!
Not Joshua Poldark. But when she died, 'e
went back to 'is old games. Chasing women
— it came natural to him. Great man was
old Joshua. 'Ard as nails. But a great man,

64

Young Cap'n. He started a line at Nampara that mustn't die out."

★ ★ ★

Two days later Tholly died. Although having a pretty good idea of the cause of death, Dwight still wanted to make sure. Tholly's only son, Lobb, the ailing, ruptured, anaemic father of five, had died last year, so Tholly's closest blood relative was his daughter, Emma Hartnell, who kept The Bounders' Arms between Sawle Church and Fernmore. Thither Dwight went to express condolences and to ask hesitantly whether he might be allowed to open the body. Cornish folk, with religious leanings and a belief in The Last Trump, generally had the strongest objection to having any relative of theirs interfered with after death by the surgeons. It came too close to the idea of the Body Snatchers. But Dwight need not have been hesitant this time. "You can have his *head* off for all I care," was the reply. Emma, though a nice woman and a kind one, had never forgiven her father for having deserted them when they were young and left them to the Poor House.

So Dwight opened up the corpse and took out the cancerous tumour and carried it home in a jar, where he could dissect it and examine its structure under a slide in his microscope. It was that part of the profession of medicine which Caroline most detested, but she had been unable to cure him of it.

He was reaching some interesting conclusions

65

on the nature of malignancy when to his annoyance Bone tapped on the door and said Music Thomas was here with the request that he should go urgently to Place House where his mistress, Mrs Valentine Warleggan, had met with a serious accident.

While Mr Pope was alive Dwight had been called not infrequently to emergencies in which the old man played the leading role, but since the young Warleggans came to live here there had been no such alarms. He went out to find Music standing on one foot and then on the other and looking anxious. Being an outdoor servant, he had no knowledge of the emergency except that he'd been told Mrs Warleggan had fallen and cut herself.

Since this *might* be a matter of life and death, Dwight grabbed up his case and swung into the saddle of the horse that had brought Music and galloped off, leaving Music to return as best he could.

He was met by Katie, who, more incoherent than usual, led him upstairs to that bedroom he knew so well, where Valentine was sitting beside Selina, who lay palely in bed, improvised bandages wrapped round both wrists.

"Ecod, it was in the bathroom," said Valentine stiffly. "I found her there. She has lost a lot of blood."

Selina was fainting, but when Dwight touched her arm she opened her Siamese-blue eyes and looked her recognition — then she closed them again.

Her wrists had been thinly cut, just where

the veins were most prominent, and blood still welled from the wounds.

Dwight sent for warm water, bathed the cuts, put a healing salve on — at which she winced — and gently bandaged both wrists, then gave her a light draught of Theban opium.

"I don't think it is very serious," he said reassuringly to Valentine, and to Selina who had sufficiently come round to swallow the draught. "Have you hurt yourself in any other way?"

She moved her lips sufficiently to say, "No."

"Did she fall?" Dwight asked Valentine, though he had a fairly good idea of the truth.

"No idea," said Valentine. "Damn me, she must have. The maid found her — Katie found her."

Dwight stayed for another ten minutes talking to Valentine and watching his client; then he rose to leave.

"I'll come down with you," said Valentine. "Martha will sit with her."

They went in to the summer parlour — which also had hardly changed since the tenure of the old man — and drank a glass of canary together. Dwight was anxious to get back to his microscope but he could not leave yet. As Valentine continued a casual conversation about Cambridge he was forced to broach the subject himself.

"I suppose you know, Mr Warleggan, that the cuts on your wife's wrists were almost certainly self-inflicted."

Valentine crossed and uncrossed his long

tapering legs. "I had that thought," he said.

Silence fell. Dwight finished his glass.

"More canary?" said Valentine.

"No, thank you. I should be on my way."

"It really is quite outrageous," Valentine said. "My wife slashed her wrists because she was told I had been with another woman." He yawned. "What is a man to do?"

"I take it her information is correct?"

"Oh yes."

After a moment Dwight said: "Well, I suppose you could refrain in future."

The young man got up and refilled Dwight's glass uninvited. Then he drank a second himself and poured out a third. "Refrain altogether? My dear Dr Enys! Isn't that being a trifle naïve?"

"It depends what you want to make of your marriage."

"This is a form of blackmail," Valentine said, squinting at his glass. "My wife threatens to kill herself in order to enforce my marriage vows! From what I could see, the cuts were not deep, were they?"

"Not deep. But a woman has to be distraught to attempt such a thing at all. And she might cut deeper next time."

"Next time. Exactly! There lies the blackmail. Behave or I will destroy myself!"

"The matter could be put in a more sympathetic light."

"No doubt. No doubt. Isn't it true, by the way, I think I have read it somewhere, that people who threaten suicide seldom succeed?"

"It's been said so. But have you ever tried to

open the veins in your own wrists? It requires a deal of resolution to go even as far as she has this time."

Valentine hunched his shoulders. "It is all such a storm in a damned tea-cup. Blood and bones, it is not civilized to behave so!"

Dwight got up. "Well, I must be off."

"No, wait. Listen. Finish that canary. You are an old friend, by God. You have known my family for thirty years. If anyone has to hear the truth why should it not be you?"

From the window Dwight saw Music Thomas coming up the track from Trevaunance. It could not have taken him all this time to walk from Killewarren.

"When I married Selina I took her for better or worse and she took me the same. Eh? Eh? I am fully committed to her, as I have frequently told her. She is mine and I want to live with her for the rest of my life! I truly want that, bubble me if I don't. Everyone at marriage makes other vows — take unto me only thyself and forsaking all others — whatever the cursed words actually are. How few even keep that vow? How few?"

"Perhaps not — "

"My only defect is my honesty. A few months after we was wed I spelt all this out to her. I told her that she was far and above the most important woman in my life but that she could not expect to be the only one. I warned her of it and warned her of it, and damn me if she could bring herself to believe it! But ever since I was breeched I have been interested in girls — can't resist 'em. At the beginning every one is different, even if at the end every one is the same! I cannot change my nature, not even for the sake of a damned peaceful married life!"

Valentine was pacing slowly about the room, his long narrow face cynically intent. Dwight sipped his wine.

"After we were married I had a couple of little affairs in Cambridge, nothing more. I imagine she knew about them. But that was over a period of *six months*! Most of the time I was as pure as a parson . . . But then when we came home for the summer vacation I met Polly Codrington. Have you met her?"

"No."

"No, I don't suppose you would have. Handsome creature, married to some dull clod of a squire in Kent — thirty years older than she is. She came to stay with Miss Darcy at Godolphin Hall. We met her, Selina and I, at the Pendarves. She was only down for a month's holiday, Polly was, and she had a roving eye. I caught it." Valentine sighed. "Mind you," he said, wishing to be reasonable with himself, "nothing blatant. We both tried to cover our tracks. Me for the reasons stated, Polly because Miss Darcy is a trifle straight in her lacing and Polly did not wish to upset the old dear. Well, we had a couple of meetings and then, not content, agreed to spend a night together at the Red Lion in Truro. I made the excuse that I wished to see my bank, she pretended she was staying with Harriet and my father — she is related to Harriet. And all went well. All went *very* well, I can tell you." Valentine licked his lips.

"I am not known in Truro. She had never been before. And then in the morning, as we were coming down the staircase together, by the worst cursed contriving of Providence, who should be passing through the hallway but that evil foul scum of a boy, Conan Whitworth. You know who I mean?"

Dwight inclined his head.

"Apparently this odious creature's school was only breaking up that day, and of course he stopped and tried to talk, but I cut him short and hurried Polly off. By then the damage was done. The fat toad must at once have hurried home and told his equally odious grandmother, who must thereupon and with great relish have proceeded to spread it about the county!"

"That does make it more difficult."

"Very much more, because you see — no doubt you do see — this hit at Selina's self-esteem. However, there it is and the milk is spilt! A mistake like this could happen to *anyone*! But, blood and bones, it is no occasion for amateur dramatics, for slashing one's *wrists* and pretending that our life together is over! Polly Codrington has now gone home to her stuffy husband in Kent and who knows if she will ever return? I am still Selina's devoted husband and intend to remain so. When you come next — you'll come tomorrow?"

"Yes."

"When you come I wish you will try to bring my wife round to some more reasonable frame of mind — and to understanding my point of view."

5

WHEN he came to leave, Katie was holding his horse. She smiled slyly at him, and he avoided looking at her thickening figure.

"Where's Music?" he asked.

"I sent him 'bout his business. He be too long coming 'ome. Wandered off, 'e had, to his own cottage I reckon, to feed all his chets."

"Don't you like cats?"

"Not so many as 'e's got."

He led his horse to the mounting stone and climbed into the saddle.

"You are keeping well, Katie?"

"Ais. Proper."

"Have you thought any more of my suggestion?"

"'Gestion?"

"That you should marry Music."

"Nay," she said. "Wouldn't do tha-at."

He smiled at her. "You have told me you do not fancy him greatly as a husband, but he might well become an excellent father."

A breeze was blowing strongly off the land, and she turned towards it so that her heavy black hair was lifted away from her face.

"'Ow do I know if he d'want to be a father to someone else's brat or no? 'E haven't said nothing to me."

Dwight's horse stamped the ground, ready to be off.

"I hear John Thomas has gone to live with Winkey and Peter Mitchell."

"Ais. He might just so well've gone years ago, mightn't 'e."

"So Music is alone in the cottage."

"'Cept for the chets. Tha's why he'm always shrimping off to feed 'em; there's no one else now. But tesn right, I d'say. Chets is independent. Chets can forage for themselves. Don't need some poor mazed man stealing time off to feed 'em."

"It is not a bad little cottage," Dwight said. "Of course it has been much neglected."

"Tis a rare old jakes."

"But could be done up, put to rights. At present there is no incentive."

"Please?"

"At present there is no one interested in it; no one to work for. Music put up some shelves for me last month. He's none too bad a man with his hands."

"Tisn't his hands that are weak," said Katie with a short laugh. "Tis his 'ead."

"Which is improving all the time. He's trying very hard, Katie. Talk to him sometime instead of shouting at him. You'd be surprised."

★ ★ ★

The following evening Katie unexpectedly had to go to the stables, and Music was there alone and put the question.

At least he mouthed something in a sweaty stutter in which the word 'wed' recurred too

74

frequently for Katie to misunderstand him.

She stared at him in contempt.

"'Ave ee been at the bottle, ye great lootal?"

"N-nay! Not so! I'm so sober as a judge. Honest! God's honour, Katie!"

"Then ye did oughter be 'shamed of yourself, thinking such lewd thoughts! *Me* wed *you*? Why I'd 'ave as much use for you as a toad for a side pocket!"

Music cringed, his knees shaking. Then with a sudden burst of bravado he said: "I dearly love bebbies. Bebbies I d'like. I dearly love the dear sweet sights."

"You've got plenty of babies," said Katie. "All them chets. Look to them." Then in vexation she added: "I d'know who's been putting you up to this monkery! Tis Surgeon Enys. Well, he'm a good man, but tis no consarn of 'is what I d'do or don't do. And tis no business of yours neether!"

"Ais, Katie," said Music humbly, and "No, Katie." And "Yes, Katie," again. He could not meet her indignant glare.

Katie would have liked at this stage to have flounced out of the stables, but she was not the flouncing sort: her step was too heavy. And, seeing the big young man looking so miserable and sweaty, she said: "Tis all well meant, I dare suppose, on both 'is side and on yourn. Who'm I to be so hoity seeing as to what I've done and the trouble that have come 'pon me? Still, there you be. Tis no more'n I desarve, and I'll tek my draught wi'out help from no one."

"I be strong," said Music, finding his voice

again. "Strong. All ways. All ways, see. God's truth. I'd labour for you and the bebby. *Tha's* no more'n you desarve."

Katie continued to stare at him from under black, contracted eyebrows.

"Giss along wi' you," she said at last. "You can't come mopping wi' me. You're 'alf saved. You know you're 'alf saved. Can't do nothing 'bout that. Even Surgeon can't. Look to your chets, Music. I'll see for myself."

★ ★ ★

As soon as Clowance heard that her father was home she had to see him. She also felt that Stephen had to go, and Stephen, still in the flush of euphoria, reluctantly agreed. They rode over and stayed two nights.

Clowance was as shocked in the appearance of her father as she had been of her mother, and the visit was a difficult one. Again Stephen was on his best behaviour and did not let his lack of interest in people a generation older than himself show in any discourteous way. He was quite fond of his mother-in-law who had continued until recently to be such a pretty woman and tolerated a father-in-law who was a distinguished man and notable in the county.

Sir Ross, it seemed, had no particular plans for his own future, and intended to live quietly for the next year or two. He had given notice that he would resign his parliamentary seat as soon as Lord Falmouth found it convenient. Lady Poldark spent most of her time in the garden, where the energy she expended was like a counter-irritant to her grief.

Isabella-Rose, fresh-faced from school, was more subdued than anyone had ever known her. Not only was she mourning for her beloved brother with whom she had had a delightful jesting relationship, but she was also deeply upset because her other beloved, Christopher Havergal, had lost a leg. After such cruelty she said she could never sing again.

After dinner on the first day, Stephen and Clowance rode over to Trenwith, but there they found only Drake and Morwenna and Loveday. Mrs Amadora Poldark had just left with her baby daughter for Paris to join her husband, who was to be stationed there as part of the army of occupation. Amadora had been over several times to see the Poldarks and had told them of her summons, but Demelza had mistaken the week she was leaving.

Then they rode on to Place House and drew a second blank. Selina was in bed with a feverish chill and had been told to see no one; Valentine was in Redruth.

In the evening Dwight and Caroline invited them all to supper, which made for a much more cheerful evening than could possibly have taken place at Nampara. Daisy and Paul Kellow had also been invited, and it was a talkative party if not a jolly one.

While carefully avoiding Waterloo, they asked a lot about the months Ross and Demelza had spent in Paris before Napoleon's escape. Ross was incredulously angry that Fouché should have now been elected President of the Provisional Government and had negotiated with the Allies for the capitulation of Paris. There was talk of his even being reappointed Chief of Police in Louis the Eighteenth's new government. "It cannot be allowed to go on!" Ross said. "This evil creature must be thrown out!"

"Perhaps Jodie will see to it in due time," Demelza said. She had had two letters recently from Mlle de la Blache, the second one from Paris, repeating an invitation that they should visit there again, now the bad time was over. Henri, Jodie thankfully reported, was safe and well. She could never thank Demelza enough for her help on that terrible escape, or be more appreciative of Isabella-Rose's innocent but vital intervention.

It was a long time since Stephen and Paul had seen each other, and the old conspirators privately exchanged congratulations, Stephen on his successful adventure at sea, Paul on his potentially successful adventure in the marriage market. They spoke of Jeremy with regret, but, being young, the thought of him being dead and dust and corruption did not so greatly worry them. Death to them was something that happened to somebody else.

Daisy, who had always had great hopes of Jeremy until he became besotted with Cuby, did not appear to repine at all. With the dreaded wasting disease having taken off two of her sisters, she lived too close to the tomb to be overawed by it.

The next day Stephen and Clowance rode

home together, Stephen feeling the satisfaction of having performed a tedious duty and the pleasure of returning to the town he had made his own and where his livelihood was always going to be. He had avoided meeting Ben, and need not now go back to the north coast for six months or more. The north coast was a backwater, a dead end, and those who lived there were welcome to it. The future lay in the Channel.

"Look you," he said, "being around and about the way I am, I hear all sorts of bits of news that don't become public till they're stale. Yesterday I heard that Coombes's cottage in Flushing was for sale. 'Member him? He worked in the Customs House. Wife died last year; he died Wednesday. Son don't want the cottage, will put it up for sale next month. Reckon if someone went along, offered seventy-five pound, quick sale, money down, he'd take it."

"Is it the one at the end of the row?"

"Next to the end. The one with the white front door. I have a mind to buy it."

"For *us*?"

"No, dear heart, not for us. The building of our house re-started last week. I thought to buy it for Andrew."

Clowance was startled. "You mean . . . "

"He's overdue now, should be home any day. He wants to get wed — he has no money. I thought to give it to them as a wedding present."

Their horses separated, and it gave her time to take in what he had said.

"Stephen, that *is* generous of you! You are so kind — I'm sure he will be delighted, overwhelmed."

"Well, he could feel aggrieved that he did not come on our venture, eh?, feel he had missed a big bonus. He can look on it that this is his share."

Clowance said: "I can't kiss you, but I will later. Thank you for such a generous thought."

Stephen laughed heartily. "And if he don't want it, I can sell it again. But I wouldn't give him the money — he might not keep it for his marriage portion!"

"I conceit Tamsin will sober him up. He'll have responsibilities. I'm told his father gambled and drank too much when he was young."

"Eh well, ye would not think so to look at him now, would ye." Stephen flicked at his horse to quicken its step. "This old nag . . . Next thing is to find me a hunter. I shall wait now till St Erme Cattle Fair in two weeks' time. They say there's some good horseflesh coming up."

"Let me come with you," said Clowance. "I haven't lived on a farm all my life for nothing."

"Wouldn't go without you," said Stephen.

They rode on.

★ ★ ★

Dwight had seen Selina the following day and then called a week later, at her request. No confidences were exchanged, and it would have been against his professional ethics to invite them. Nor, had she told him the facts, would he have been prepared to put Valentine's point of view. On this third visit, when he found her up and about, she spoke rather sheepishly of her clumsiness in breaking the glasses, and attempted to demonstrate to him how she had fallen forward, cutting both wrists at the same time. The amount of blood she had lost was little, and the dark rings under her eyes were no doubt concerned with the cause of the accident, not the accident itself.

He sat chatting for a few minutes, discussing the arrival off Plymouth of the Emperor Napoleon Bonaparte as a prisoner of the British in HMS *Bellerophon*. Selina was of the opinion that he was being treated with too great a respect — it was said that every officer, English and French, uncovered when he came on deck and that the harbour was swarming with small boats trying to get a glimpse of him. Dwight said he was not sure as to the amount of respect he deserved. It was true that, but for him, many thousands of good young men — including one very near and dear to them all — would be alive. But it was the custom of the British to show respect for their fallen enemies and, as well as being a terrible scourge, which everyone admitted, Bonaparte was a great man. For instance the Civil Code which he had introduced into France would probably provide a model for future generations.

On this Valentine arrived, having been out riding. Conversation abruptly lagged, and then

Selina, smiling too brightly at Dwight, asked to be excused.

After she had gone Valentine said: "Not drinking? My wife has caught some of the parsimonious habits of her former husband. I swear you did not like the canary you had before. This is a very good Mountain, shipped direct from Malaga. Try a glass."

Dwight tried a glass, and for a while talk continued on the subject of the late Emperor.

Then Valentine said: "Tell me, Dr Enys. What did my mother die of?"

Dwight thought cautiously round the sudden change of subject: "She died in childbirth. Your sister — "

"Ursula was born on the 10th of December. My mother did not die until the 14th."

"It is not uncommon, if something goes amiss, for the mother to survive a few days."

"Do you know what went amiss?"

"She died of blood poisoning," said Dwight shortly.

"Was that why she smelt so bad?"

Dwight looked up, startled.

Valentine said: "Well, you see, I was nearly six at the time. They would not let me into her room but the smell escaped into the passage. It is a smell I have never been able to forget."

There was an uneasy silence. Dwight said: "I am sorry you were allowed near. The disagreeable smell was due to a putrid condition of the blood."

Valentine resumed his ramshackle pacing. "You will excuse these questions, Dr Enys, but you have been a friend of the family, and their physician, long before I was born and you must know more about my family than almost anyone alive."

"I have known your family for thirty years but I have not been their physician. Your father always had the Truro man, Dr Behenna, and he was engaged to wait on your mother when Ursula was born. I was called in because labour began prematurely while she was still at Trenwith."

"Prematurely?"

"Yes."

"I too was a premature baby. Eight months, I understand."

"I understand so."

"And so became the cause of great dissension between my father and my mother."

"I do not know what gave you that impression."

"A six-year-old boy is not without perception, especially where his parents are concerned."

"No. Maybe not. But . . . "

"It is good, this wine, isn't it," said Valentine. "My wife's money enables me to live off the fat of the land, so no doubt a more moral man than I am would feel obliged to adhere more obviously to his marriage vows."

"That is for you to decide — "

"I wonder if my mother adhered to her marriage vows?"

Dwight finished his wine and got up. "I don't think I can help you on this subject, Mr Warleggan."

83

"You cannot have lived in these villages for so long without knowing that nothing is ever kept permanently secret. My problem is remembering what I knew in my heart as a child and what I have heard in sidelong whispers since. What I do know . . . Pray sit down again."

Dwight reluctantly sat on the edge of a chair but waved away an attempt to refill his glass. He appreciated that under the surface gloss Valentine was speaking of something that had been gathering a long time in his heart.

"As a child I soon came to see that I was the bone of contention between my parents. Sometimes all would be apparently well, and then a word would be dropped, a shadow of some sort would be cast — and it always involved me. Sometimes for a month at a time my father would not speak to me, would not even look at me. I might have been some leprous monstrosity which had to be ignored and shunned. Unclean! Unclean! Of course my mother was not like that. Her loving care for me never wavered . . . Naturally all this did not make for a happy childhood."

"I'm sorry."

"Did you know that my parents had a violent quarrel only a day or two before Ursula was born?"

"No, I did not."

"D'ye know, I have a pretty clear memory of the events of December '99. We had been in London and rather happy there. At least, my mother seemed to be, and that reflected on me. She had got much fatter, and I did

84

not understand that, but my father was in a good mood and I was happy with some new toys. I remember specially a rocking horse. I wonder what happened to that? Suddenly it all changed — as it had done sometimes in the past, but never so badly as this — and I felt I was guilty of some terrible sin. We journeyed back to Cornwall, and I remember I was coachsick most of the way. It is not at all agreeable, my dear Dr Enys, being coachsick at the best of times, but when your father looks his utter disgust — indeed hatred — at every fresh retch . . .

"When we reached Truro influenza, scarlet fever and dysenteries were raging, so my mother took me off to Trenwith to see her parents and to keep me out of infection's way. Smelter George stayed behind. It was a dark month. Do you remember it at all?"

"Very well."

"Trenwith was monstrous dark. It might have been haunted. Do you remember the great storm that blew up during that first week?"

"Yes."

"It was one of the worst storms that had ever been, but, child-like, I found it vastly exciting. The servants we had, Tom and Bettina — d'you know; I cannot remember their surnames — they took me out to see the sea at Trevaunance; they got a good wigging afterwards for taking me, for roofs were blowing off and branches falling. But suddenly at supper that night my father turned up with a face like fury. I was so excited out of my usual fear of him that I tried to tell him about the storm. He snapped back at me as if I were an evil thing, and I was sent instantly to bed — in something of a temper myself, I may say."

Valentine picked a piece of ore off the mantelshelf, weighed it appreciatively in his hand. "Early assays on Wheal Elizabeth are promising — copper very obvious, but signs also of tin and zinc."

"Very promising."

"That night," said Valentine, "after I had been put to bed and the candle blown out, I got up again and padded along to my mother's bedroom. But I did not go in. My parents were both there and in the midst of one of their bitterest quarrels. I listened to it all, taking in words but not comprehending them. Only since. Only since, remembering the words, have I gathered their meaning. It seemed that George Warleggan thought he was not my father."

Dwight frowned. "Are you sure you remembered the words correctly, that you did not misinterpret the causes of the quarrel? Children can so often mistake these things."

"Do you mean to tell me that you have never heard whispered doubts in these villages about my parentage?"

"There is always tittle-tattle in villages, Mr Warleggan. Most of it is entirely invented and should be ignored."

Valentine pushed back his hair. His vivid eccentric manner was at odds with this rather stuffy room, furnished by his elderly predecessor.

"When Ursula was born George Warleggan

came into my bedroom to tell me. I was terrified
— he had never been into my room for as long as
I could remember. But now — for some reason
— it was as if the storm — his storm — had
passed. He actually patted my hand, told me
about my sister, said that my mother was well
but must rest in bed for a few days. He talked
to me about going to school, about the recent
gale, almost as if no enmity had existed between
us. I could make nothing of it, remained frozen
to his touch. Children cannot change as quickly
as all that. I was relieved when he left. I only
wanted to see my mother again. This, of course,
I did, and also Ursula, but the day after that my
mother was taken ill — and the day after that
she died."

Through the open window you could hear the
children calling to their cattle in the fields. A
horse whinnied in the nearby stables.

Dwight said: "Your mother was delivered
prematurely of a perfectly healthy child. I
delivered the child. I did not see your mother
again for two days, as Dr Behenna arrived and
took charge. Then when I was called in again
I was appalled at the sight of her illness. Do
not misunderstand me, this could not have been
the result of any mistaken treatment Dr Behenna
prescribed. Had I seen the complaint earlier I
would have diagnosed it more quickly, but could
not have halted it."

"And the complaint was?"

"I have told you. A form of blood poisoning."

"Gangrene, wasn't it? I have read books."

"A form of blood poisoning."

"Caused by what?"

Dwight thought: almost certainly by drinking part of the contents of a little bottle I still have in my cupboard at home. He had no means of analysing it, but he had tasted it and could make a reasonable guess at some of the ingredients. But never could he say anything of this to any human being, least of all to Elizabeth's son.

"Dr Behenna described it as an acute gouty condition of the abdominal viscera which manifested itself in cramp-like spasms and inhibition of the nerve fluids."

"Do you believe all that medical flummery? You are, after all, well known to be the most advanced and knowledgeable physician in the south-west."

Dwight stared at the tensed-up young man. "However knowledgeable any one of us is, we struggle in the dark, Mr Warleggan. We know so little of the human body, even after centuries of practice and experience."

He might have added: And of the mind, Mr Warleggan, and of the mind.

6

ELLERY and Vigus had dropped hints about it at the changing of the cores, though they hadn't dared to face him out. But Peter Hoskin was a more substantial character and when he made a sort of side reference to it he tackled him in the changing shed.

"Well, I dunno narthing 'bout en," said Peter. "'Tis only what I been telled. Beth Daniel fur one. And others. But it edn naught to do wi' me, Ben."

"If it edn't naught to do wi' you," said Ben, "why don't ee keep yer big trap shut!"

"I don't see as you've any call to take on so," said Peter testily. "Why don't ee ask her? She'll soon tell ee nay if tedn truth."

Katie was normally home on Tuesday afternoon, that being her afternoon off; though she had seen much less of her parents' shop since her disgrace. Jinny, her mother, being a good and respectable Wesleyan, had not taken kindly to a situation in which her daughter should now be preparing to bear a bastard child without making any attempt to bring the scoundrel to justice who was responsible for her condition.

Ben went along and found Katie at home helping her mother to cut up the rhubarb for jam.

Whitehead Scoble, their step-father, was now

very deaf and was dominated by Jinny who, though of a naturally amiable disposition, had hardened and toughened with the years.

"Well," said Katie defiantly, "what if tis true? Tis my consarn, no one's else."

"Lord save us!" said Ben between his teeth, "ye cann't mean it, Katie. Ye cann't. Wed to the village idiot! For land's sake, don't that beat all!"

"I don't see you need to get in such a niff," said Katie. "He's not such a noodle as he belonged to be. Ye give a man a name and it d'hang round his neck like a dog collar all 'is life. Besides . . ."

"Besides what?"

"I've the child to think on."

"'E'll thank ye, sure 'nough, 'e truly will — or she — to be give a father that don't know the time o' day or whether tis Christmas or Easter! If you wed a pattick like Music ye'll have to keep three 'stead of two — "

"He've got a cottage."

"Oh, so you're wedden the cottage, are ee — "

"I never said that! I never said nothing o' the sort . . . Anyway, tis my life and I shall lead it as I think fit — "

"But tis not fitty. Wi' all the village a-sniggering to bust. They're whispering and sniggering at the mine already. Why, folk'll jeer at you, not at him — "

"Oh, leave the maid alone," said Jinny. "She've dug her own pit — let her lie in it!"

"What's that?" said Whitehead. "What's that

you say?" He began to light his nose warmer from a spill thrust between the bars of the fire. A cloud of smoke from the shag drifted across the room.

"You mean t'say you don't *mind*?" Ben turned on his mother.

"Course I mind! But I mind the disgrace the more. If I had my way I'd have that Saul Grieves fetched back from wherever he be skulking and *forced* into church. What he did with his self after that would be his consarn. But this way he d'get off fine and free and leave Katie to bear the consequences!"

"I've told ee," Katie said, near to tears but not giving way. "I'd never marry Saul Grieves, not if he was to come on bended knee. Music's just a makeshift. But twill make the child legal and give him a name."

"Well, don't expect *me* to acknowledge Music as me brother-in-law! You must be half saved yerself, Katie, to think on such a thing. What do Grandfather and Grandmother say? They'll spit. I reckon they'll spit."

Jinny came across to him. "Don't you go upsetting Granfer and Gran, else I'll give you something to think 'bout, Ben! They're old, and when the time d'come I'll go and tell 'em what I think best they should know. But until then, you keep your spleen to yourself!"

"They'll know about it soon enough," said Ben. "You'll find some kind friend'll be along any day, if mebbe they don't already know. Anyway, I'd not like to be there when you d'tell 'em!"

He left the room, and they heard the shop door slam as he went out.

"What was amiss with him?" asked Whitehead. "He was in a rare taking. I suppose he don't like the idea of Katie wedding Music?"

* * *

Andrew Blamey returned in the *Queen Charlotte* after a stormy voyage which had taken twice as long as expected and in which they had been attacked by, and driven off, a big American privateer that had not yet apparently become aware of the Peace Treaty of Ghent. He accepted Stephen's gift of the cottage with uproarious pleasure, and they celebrated it at a little supper-party in the Carringtons' cottage, Tamsin being there chaperoned by her brother George. Consent to the marriage by her parents had not yet been given, but everyone at the supper assumed it would only be a matter of time.

Grown expansive on the Rhenish wine, Stephen went into more details of his privateering escapade than Clowance had heard before. In particular when the French soldier had fired point blank at him and the cap had failed to detonate. Stephen now treated it as a great joke, but it had been the luckiest escape from certain death. Clowance could not help but think of another and longer conflict, and wish that the rain had continued at Waterloo.

It seemed that Andrew had enjoyed his trip in the *Queen Charlotte*. In spite of his joviality, Andrew was not the easiest of men to get on with, and so it was notable that he had found an accord with the grumpy Captain Buller. Something in Andrew's character had responded to the stern discipline of his captain, and something in the way he had responded had pleased and satisfied Buller. The success of the voyage radiated through Andrew's spirits, and though he drank plenty he did not become noticeably drunk. They made gay plans for a day next week when they would visit the new cottage together.

On the Friday Stephen and Clowance rode out to St Erme, whose annual cattle and horse fair was the biggest in the county, and Stephen paid what Clowance thought an outrageous price for a handsome dark bay gelding, 'the property of an officer recently fallen at Waterloo'. The two men selling the horse told Stephen that they would get a far better price at Tattersall's but they were selling locally to avoid the cost of the travelling. Moses, as he was called, was a very big animal — seventeen hands — and was clearly accustomed to hunting. A six-year-old, they said, and Stephen could not take his eyes off it. As well as being good at persuading himself that what he wanted was right, he had a similar tendency to believe the persuasiveness of others; and the sale was soon completed.

They rode through Truro and back to Falmouth in triumph, Clowance on Nero leading the hired horse. Even if he has paid too much for it, she thought, it's his money, won by his enterprise, why shouldn't he have the enjoyment? Just as he enjoyed giving me the necklace. Just as he has enjoyed giving the cottage to Andrew. (I hope he has as much money as he says. I hope — I do hope and pray — he will know when to say stop.)

★ ★ ★

The courtship of Music and Katie did not follow a conventional pattern.

For one thing, they did not look at each other as affianced people should. Music gazed constantly at Katie, his pale puzzled eyes gleaming with happiness — he was in his seventh heaven only because there was not an eighth — but he never let his gaze fall below her face. He became alert and experienced in interpreting the nuances of her expressions — which boded ill for him, which tolerance, which — very rarely — liking or approval. He never allowed his gaze to travel anywhere below her chin, for he knew without ever having been told that her corporeal presence lower than the neck was not for him. It was unthinkable territory.

For her part, although she quite frequently spoke to him, she always kept her eyes lowered, as if to reduce within herself the shame of such a match. To meet his adoring eyes would have been to establish a contact, an intimacy which could, of course, never be allowed to establish itself. She went to his cottage, walked around it, made comments, a few suggestions, which he eagerly agreed to. In the end she found he only had four cats. Tom, one of the scabby tabby toms, had been caught in a gin at the beginning of the year, so all that were left were Tabby, Ginger, Blackie and Whitey, which was certainly more than she wanted, but Music was so obviously devoted to them that she decided to tolerate them. In the harsh cat world of Grambler, wastage would no doubt take one or another off in due time, so long as she was absolutely firm about admitting newcomers.

Music went about in a dream world, working every spare moment he could get away from Place House, which was little enough, putting new thatch on part of the roof, clearing out the smelly fishing-tackle, hanging the back door on new hasps so that it would shut properly, mending the broken windows, repairing the fire bars, cleaning out the jakes and laying stones to it across the dusty scrub of the yard. In his excitement he had to be careful not to walk on his toes again or let his voice break into its upper register.

One day when he was trying to repair the table leg his older brother John walked in. He had come over to see what was going on. They were neither of them men of many words, and after a few grunted monosyllables of greeting John spat on the floor and thrust his hands into the upper pockets of his breeches and watched Music trying to get the table to stand steady without rocking.

"When'll ye wed?" he asked presently.

"Dunno."

"I've 'erd tell tis to be the 1st October."

"Mebbe."

"What Katie says goes, eh?"

"Mebbe." Music stopped to scowl at his table. "Ais, I reckon. What Katie says goes."

"Know ye she's only marryin' ye on account that she's forced put?"

"I reckon."

"It don't fret ye that ee be going to be fathur to Saul Grieves's child?"

"Tes Katie's child. That's for sure."

"Aye, that's for sure. What do Art say?"

"'Aven't asked 'im."

"Nay, ye wouldn't. Well, I tell ee what ee d'say. He say you'm all mops an' brooms where Katie's consarned. She cares for you no more than for a pail of muggets. Tis just convenience. That's what tis, Music. Just convenience."

Music stretched up. "Aye?"

"Aye. He also d'say, and tis the very truth of the matter, that we all three on us own part o' this yur cottage. So if you be gwan set up house wi' this woman and 'ave her child, tis no more'n right 'n proper that you d'pay a rent to we."

"What?"

John Thomas repeated his words, aware that Music was not taking them in. Eventually Music said: "You mun ast Katie."

"Aye, I thought so much. Ast Katie. She'll run ee round like a cocket, I'll tell ee for certain, I sorrow for ee, Music. I sorrow for ee."

"Ais?" Music smiled. "Well I bain't sorrowing for meself, see?"

After a few weeks the whispering and the sniggering died down, and people began to accept the match. Music, though a big strong young man, was weak-willed and easily sat on and very sensitive to ridicule. Katie was a big strong young girl, not at all weak-willed, and, when she was among her own kind, a formidable presence. Folk didn't laugh in her face and she cared little for what was said behind her back. Also there was the distant Poldark connection. Her brother was underground captain of Wheal Grace and Wheal Leisure. Her mother had worked for the Poldarks for a long time, a long time ago, and so had her father. Her grandfather, Zacky Martin, who had been a semi-invalid for years, had been Cap'n Poldark's right-hand man through the early troublous years and still lived in Mellin, hard by Nampara. An uncle and an aunt, no older than she was, were employed at Nampara, in the house and on the farm.

It counted for something in the village. It made the enormity of the match greater but it made criticism of it more subdued.

A conversation concerning it took place that evening at Nampara where Demelza, for the first time since her return, had Dwight and Caroline to supper. For this evening only Isabella-Rose had been asked if she would have supper upstairs.

"It is not that we have anything private to discuss that we don't wish you to hear," Demelza said to her. "It is just that we are four old friends, of an age; we have not met like this for so long. We would feel the same if Clowance were here or — or anyone else."

Bella kissed her. "One day I shall be grown

97

up and then I shall have nothing more to do with you."

They ate a piece of fresh salmon, fricasseed rabbits, a blackcurrant pie and syllabubs, with cherries after. At one time Demelza had been a little on edge even when entertaining such old friends; now perhaps her stay in Paris and later at Lansdowne House made things easier; one didn't worry about a servant's gaffe. Or perhaps it was that one no longer cared.

The meal went easily and pleasantly; the room became a little corner of comfort in a black world.

Mention of Zacky Martin brought it up. Ross said Zacky was scandalized and upset by his granddaughter's disgrace, and now by her crazy decision to marry the village idiot.

"He's by no means that," Dwight said, sharply for him. "In fact he never was. Slow-witted and amiable, certainly, and at one time he rather enjoyed being the butt of the village. It was a sort of fame. But in the last few years he's been trying to grow out of it."

"Dwight has been very good to him," said Caroline. "Spent hours with him."

"Half an hour a week at most," said Dwight. "But he came and asked what was wrong with him. I was surprised. Village idiots, as they are called, don't usually realize there is anything wrong with themselves; they think it is other people who are at fault. So I thought I would spend an hour or two testing his capacities. I found nothing wrong, physically. He has a good alto voice — but so have other normal people.

98

When he was a child one of his brothers pushed him into the fire and he burnt his feet, chiefly his heels. He got into the habit of walking on his toes, but now he has got out of it. Mentally he's slow. But so are a number of his friends. Recently he has learned to count, and if he concentrates he can tell the time. He knows the months of the year now, and he's good with animals and clever with his hands. It may not be a lot, but I think he is sufficiently normal to have the right to live a normal life."

"I suspicion that Dwight has been the matchmaker," said Demelza.

"I'm not guiltless. But in this company . . . It is likely that Caroline and I would never have come together again if it had not been for that man's interference."

"It's too long ago," said Ross. "I deny responsibility. But if it comes to matchmaking, Demelza is in the forefront of us all."

"Well," said Demelza, and blew a cherry stone genteelly into her fist, "that's as maybe. But d'you know, the one I regret was the match I *didn't* make. Betwixt my brother Sam and Emma Tregirls, as she then was. There was such a gap — Sam's religion, you know — so I suggested they should part for a year . . . Emma went to Tehidy. But before the year was up she married the footman there, Hartnell, and so it was too late for Sam's happiness."

"He's happy married now," said Ross. "So is Emma. I do not think it could ever have worked . . . But seriously, Dwight, if you think well of Music Thomas, I wish you might find time to

99

call and see Zacky and Mrs Zacky. They would take greater notice of what you said, and it might set their minds more easy."

"I will. I would take Music with me, but I know he would be so sweatily nervous that he would show to the worst advantage."

"If ee please, mum," said Betsy Maria Martin, of that ilk, coming in. "Henry d'say you promised to go up and tell him good-night."

"So I did," said Demelza. "I'll come in five minutes."

Supper was all but over, but they stayed round the table chatting in the desultory way that Demelza so enjoyed. Caroline had sent her two daughters to an expensive school in Newton Abbot but she was not satisfied with it and was considering keeping them at home again and employing a teacher-governess.

"We want someone like your Mrs Kemp," said Caroline. "Someone with a rod, if not of iron, at least of birch, to stop Dwight spoiling them."

"Oh Mrs Kemp was wonderful in Paris," said Demelza. "She was a rock. But do not suppose that she is so highly educated that she would suit for Sophie and Meliora. Have you asked Mrs Pelham's advice?"

"Oh my dear darling aunt is at last showing signs of age, and although she loves to have us all there I do not think she would willingly undertake the semi-permanent custody of my two lanky brats."

"I wasn't thinking that. I was thinking she might know someone. You need someone more

100

like Morwenna, who was so good with Geoffrey Charles."

They sipped their port. Then Demelza rose.

"Well, I suppose I must not keep Henry waiting."

"The future Sir Harry," said Caroline.

"Yes, that's so."

"Though I trust a long way in the future. And always I suppose subject to whether Cuby's child is a boy or a girl."

"Oh?" said Demelza. "Oh, yes."

"Have you heard from Cuby?" Dwight asked Ross.

"I think she plans to come down next month."

★ ★ ★

In bed that night Demelza said: "Is that true, what Caroline said about Cuby's baby?"

"What was that?"

"That if it should be a boy, he would inherit the title, not Henry."

"Yes, I suppose so. Does it matter?"

Demelza thought it over.

Ross said: "It is of little moment to me that I should have a title to pass on. Do you care?"

"I'm not sure, Ross. I think I do. I certainly care that you have a title, as you know. And Cuby's son is your grandson, and it would be well enough if he inherited. But . . . I think that Henry is your *son*, and it would be more proper for him to have it."

"Maybe. I hadn't thought. It is not important.

101

Anyway nature will make up its own mind."

The window was open on the warm night, and a moth flew in. It began to make perilous circuitous reconnaissances round the candle.

"Old Maggie Dawe used to call 'em meggyhowlers," said Demelza.

"What? Oh, did she? That's a name even Jud didn't know."

"Have you seen him since you came home?"

"No. I must go tomorrow."

"I went early on, but it was in the first shock and I do not suppose I was as attentive to their complaints as usual."

After a pause Ross said: "Did you know that Cuby was in Cornwall?"

"No! Is she coming here?"

"I avoided a direct answer when Caroline asked. Cuby promised to come here for the birth of her child, but that is three months off. She is staying at Caerhays with her family."

"Oh."

"She did not mention it when I left her. Perhaps there has been a change of plan."

"Who told you?"

"I saw John-Evelyn Boscawen in Truro yesterday. He knew Jeremy well, of course. They were of an age. He assumed I knew about Cuby."

Demelza thought this over too. "I think she might have written."

"Perhaps she will."

"She was some nice to me when I was in Brussels."

"She may feel a few weeks at home will be

102

good for her first. She was still in a state of shock."

"We all are."

"Indeed."

"Shall you go over and see her, Ross?"

"Oh no. I think the decision to communicate with us must come from her. We must give her time."

"Time," said Demelza. "Yes, I suppose we all have lots of time . . . "

In the warm night you could hear the thunder of the sea on the beach. It was there almost all the time but only on quiet nights did it penetrate to one's consciousness. "*Rum-a-dum-dum*," said Ross to himself. "*Rum-a-dum-dum.*" Pray God that sound would never be heard again.

"What were you muttering?" Demelza asked.

"I was cursing under my breath."

"What for?"

"Because I have to get up and push your meggyhowler out of the window. Its suicidal tendencies will prevent me from going to sleep."

"Put out the candle."

"Then it will flutter round our faces in the dark."

"Looking for another flame," said Demelza.

7

MOSES was a good mount. He was mettlesome and took some controlling at first but after a week or so he took to his new owner. Stephen was not the easiest of riders: he didn't really know how to gentle a horse along, persuading him instead of ordering him, he didn't talk to him enough. (When Clowance, the unloquacious, rode with Nero alone she talked to him all the time.) But they came to understand each other. It is probable that Moses' former owner, if he was a cavalry officer as well as a huntsman, had treated his horse well, ridden it hard, and lacked finesse. If so Moses, who had a hard mouth, recognized a new and similar-minded master. "Geldings always make the best jumpers," Stephen said.

He was delighted. He was noticeable on this horse wherever he went. He temporarily neglected his shipping interests and galloped each morning with Clowance over the moors west of Falmouth. He couldn't wait for the next hunting season to begin. He couldn't wait to show his horse to Harriet.

An opportunity for this occurred earlier than he had expected. Sid Bunt had put in to Penryn, and after reporting and checking his stores he was off with the *Lady Clowance* like the delivery van he was, to complete a half-dozen commissions up the Fal.

Most of these were workaday, but the big house at Trelissick had ordered a harp and two paintings, two late Opies — the painter had been dead several years but his work was becoming still more prized. Stephen was interested enough to see that these all travelled well, and in the ordinary course of events, if he had been free of his other vessels, he would have sailed with the *Lady Clowance* as far as King Harry Ferry for the off-loading. This time, because he was so proud of his horse, he rode overland to meet the *Lady Clowance* there. He superintended the landing of the cargo and met the owner of the house and took a glass of sherry with him before he started for home, full of the satisfaction of having made one more influential acquaintance.

Trelissick is not far from Cardew but it is separated from it by the Carnon Stream. Having dropped down to stream level and crossed by the old bridge, he let Moses amble along at his own pace enjoying the sunshine and the warm air. On impulse he turned into Carnon Wood, remembering the hunt had once taken them through there, and the hair-raising ride — almost literally hair-raising — they had had among the low branches. The wood was not above twenty acres in extent but it had only one decent path through it and a clearing with a workman's hut, part ruined, in the middle. At an earlier season the ground was ablaze with bluebells and wild daffodils. Rabbits abounded and lots of game — hares, badgers, woodcock, snipe.

As he came into the clearing he saw a woman pacing cautiously round the perimeter. She was tall and well dressed, in a purple riding cap and waistcoat with nankeen-coloured skirt, worn short enough to show purple shoes and embroidered stockings. It was Lady Harriet Warleggan. Her rich black hair was in a queue. She carried a riding crop.

"Harriet!" called Stephen in surprise.

She stopped and looked at him, scowling into the sun. At first she did not look well pleased as he rode up and dismounted, taking off his hat.

"Well, well, so it is our conquering hero!"

"What a vastly agreeable surprise!" he said, taking her gloved hand. "I had not hoped to meet you here — and out walking in your . . ."

He hesitated. Because she was tall and well built, her figure only just showed the child she carried.

"In my present condition, you were going to say?"

"Well, me dear, maybe I should just say I'm gratified to find ye out walking."

"I shall be out walking for some time yet. Being in whelp is not so disabling as I supposed it was going to be. But do not be concerned: Nankivell is at the edge of the wood, holding Dundee for me. Also Castor and Pollux. I am well mounted and well escorted."

It was not in Stephen's nature ever to feel awkward — it was one of his charms — and he explained his presence here and what he had been doing this morning and asked her what she was seeking in the wood.

"Foxes," she said simply. "We cannot hunt 'em for two months yet, and by then, God dammit, I shall be too far on to participate. But I can still keep an eye on 'em, see what cubs they have. Even if you can't catch 'em at play you can usually tell by the billet they leave. You've spoiled my quest, Master Carrington."

"I'm not sure I follow."

"Simple enough. Why else do I leave my escort a quarter of a mile away? It is not the exercise of walking that I so much enjoy. But I had hopes I might see one or two of my little friends and gauge their health and numbers. That is not best done in the company of two clumping horses and a brace of boarhounds."

Stephen laughed. "Well, since I've spoiled a part of your quest, can I not help ye with the other part of it?"

"What is that?"

"Counting the droppings."

She smiled at this. He tethered Moses to a suitable tree.

"A fine horse," she said.

"Aye," said Stephen, bridling. "I wished for ye to see him. Something I bought last week in St Erme. He is quite a special animal."

"A bit heavy in the hindquarters, do you not think?"

"Nay, tis the breed, Harriet. And he has a fair weight to carry."

They moved towards the hut, but Harriet turned off sharply to where there was a rift in the ground and a couple of gorse bushes, still in semi-flower.

"You see, there's an earth here. Badgers have made it but foxes are living in it. I'll lay a curse there's a handsome lot of cubs in there. I was hoping to catch 'em at play."

"I'm in disgrace, eh?"

"No matter." She allowed the gorse bush to fall back into place and brushed some prickles off her gloves. "We'll look in this hut and then be done."

They walked across the clearing.

"How is Clowance?"

"Well and fine, thank ee."

"She must have been much upset by her brother's death."

"Oh she was. So was I. Jeremy was a sterling fellow."

"I gather that while he was fighting Napoleon you were fighting the French in a more profitable way."

He glanced at her and laughed. "You speak the truth. I had me narrow escapes, I can vow. But, thanks to you, I got the opportunity to make the venture."

"Thanks to me?"

"Well, ye must know that Sir George and I fell out — or maybe it is more true to say that he soured of me for some reason and threatened to withdraw all credit. I was as good as a ruined man. Then, for some other reason, he changed his mind and allowed me to continue to function on restricted credit. Twas that that brought me to a situation

108

where I had to go for all or nothing as a privateer."

"Indeed," said Harriet at the entrance of the hut, "so that's how it was."

"That's how it was. And I have *you* to thank for it."

"I am at a loss to know why you should think so."

"I b'lieve Clowance told ye something of our straits and that ye intervened with Sir George on my behalf."

"What a quaint thought!" She led the way into the hut.

It was a wooden structure, with part of the roof gone and the door fallen in. Inside there was a lot of etiolated grass, a few brambles, some small bones, ashes from a fire.

Harriet stirred the grass with her foot. "Some tramp has been sharing it with the foxes."

"Foxes?"

"Oh, they'll come in places like this, especially if their earths have been stopped. We have been led this way more than once and the scent has gone cold. I wonder . . . "

"I mind once last year," said Stephen, "last December, we came this way, dashing through the wood. I nearly came off! As usual, you was in the front."

"Dundee is very sure-footed. And we've been together a long time; since before I married George. We don't often make mistakes in the field."

"Was your first husband a great hunter?"

"Oh yes, he lived for it. He was Master for a

time, not of this pack, of course, but in North Devon. Nearly ruined himself — and in the end broke his neck at a gate. Well, God rest his soul, it was as good a way as any to go."

Stephen had not been alone with this cool, articulate, downright woman in quite this way before. She was physically very attractive; pregnancy had given her an extra bloom. She had never spoken so openly and personally. It excited him.

She was stooping, stirring over the bones with her crop. He bent beside her, aware of her perfume, of her queue of black hair, of the flush in her normally sallow cheek.

"Do you see anything?"

"These rabbit bones are new. And these are chicken bones and something bigger. Mme Vixen has been sharing her vittles with someone else." She straightened up, and he straightened up beside her.

"Harriet."

"Yes?"

"Twas your doing, was it not, keeping George from bankrupting me? Don't deny it. I have to thank ye."

"Is it not better to forget it all? Or why do you not give George the credit?"

"Because it is *yours* and I have to thank ye."

She had her back near the wall, and he put a hand on the wall each side of her, imprisoning her. The wooden shack creaked under the weight of his hands.

She looked at him coldly, great eyes very calm.

110

He kissed her, first on the cheek and then on the lips. It was a long kiss. Then she put hands on both his shoulders and pushed him away. It was slow but firm; she had strong arms.

She took out a handkerchief and dabbed her lips. Then she picked up her crop, which she had dropped and stooped to turn over the bones again.

"I heard a parson once in the pulpit," she said, "state that man was the only creature that killed for pleasure. Damned nonsense. A fox will kill anything that moves, that flutters, that shows signs of life. So will a cat. So will a leopard. Foxes are nasty little brutes, but I love 'em."

"I can kill things that flutter," said Stephen.

He followed her out of the hut.

"I think we will rejoin Nankivell."

Stephen unhitched Moses and followed the tall smart woman through the trees. They came out into the field beyond, where the little groom was waiting with two horses and two dogs. Nankivell got to his feet, taking off his hat; the two big boarhounds rose and stretched and made whining noises. Harriet did not have to bend in order to rub their ears.

"Nankivell, take the dogs back by the road. It will do them good to trot with you. Mr Carrington and I will canter back across country."

"'S, m'lady."

Harriet put out a hand and Nankivell helped her mount. The two horses, Dundee and Moses, eyed each other. Harriet gathered her reins, adjusted her cap. She had not looked at Stephen since they came out of the hut.

"Well, be off with you."

"'S, m'lady. Beg pardon, m'lady, but Sir George did tell me to see as ee did not go cross-country galloping. He says to me, Sir George he says, mind you see her leddyship don't do any jumping or galloping — "

"Never mind what Sir George said. It is what I say. Mr Carrington will see me home."

"Willingly," said Stephen.

"That's if he can keep up with me."

In silence they watched Nankivell mount and trot reluctantly off, with Castor and Pollux on long leads behind. It was obviously a routine the dogs were used to. Stephen was still standing beside his horse, but now he essayed to mount. Harriet watched with a critical eye as he struggled into the saddle.

It was not so warm out here. The wind was picking up from the east, and they were not sheltered by the trees. But Stephen was warm.

Harriet said: "If you wish to know, I did influence Sir George in his decision not to withdraw banking credit from you. But I did it for Clowance, not for you. To suppose that I am in any way interested in you as a man is an unwarranted assumption. I have a debt of friendship and gratitude towards Clowance, which I discharged. That is all."

Stephen patted his horse's neck. "Maybe I've a debt of friendship and gratitude towards you just the same. Maybe once in a while you'll let me show it."

Harriet said: "Your horse is heavy in the

112

haunches. If you're not careful he'll grow fat. I know the type."

"I reckon he's a wonderful horse," said Stephen stiffly. "Every bit so good as yours."

Harriet tightened her reins and looked across the smiling summer countryside.

She said after a long pause: "When you married Clowance, it was a big thing for you, Stephen. Be content with it. I do not think it time for you to consider moving farther up-stream. Good-day to you."

She turned and went off at a fair pace, which soon turned into a gallop.

"C'mon, me lad," said Stephen angrily. "We'll catch her."

He set Moses to the task, and for a short period gained on her. It was uphill and the bigger horse made ground. Then Harriet took a low hedge very gracefully and Stephen followed. Now it was level ground and the two horses galloped at about the same rate, Moses some three lengths behind.

Another hedge, a Cornish wall this, not higher but much broader. Over went Dundee. Moses dislodged a stone as he followed. Harriet looked behind and laughed. Stephen dug in his heels and whacked the hindquarters of his horse with his crop. It was lovely open country, between wooded slopes and tall individual trees. They were galloping now at a thunderous pace.

He knew she should not be galloping like this, and knew that if he halted she would probably slow down. But he could not bring himself to check his horse. Harriet's words had bitten

113

into him like a serpent, the poison seeping and spreading. She had even sneered at his horse.

He knew he must overtake her soon and then, having caught her, he could slow her down and be magnanimous. His horse was bigger than hers and must have more staying power; besides, a woman, unless she is a dare-devil, cannot ride side-saddle at the speed of a man. Harriet was a dare-devil. She bobbed up and down, her queue of hair streaming behind her. Now for the first time she used her whip.

They were coming to the next obstacle. Woods on either side narrowed to a gap protected by a high fence. Beyond it was a deep ditch. Harriet half checked, then slapped Dundee's neck; the horse took a sort of double stammer of hooves and took the obstacle in huge style. He just landed in the rubble and stones on the far side, stumbled and came to his feet as Stephen prepared to take off.

Stephen had been nearer Harriet than he thought; their hesitation, which had really been only a gathering of muscle and determination for the leap, became in him a real hesitation; then he forced Moses forward with a stinging crack of his whip and the great horse took off half a stride early. He made a tremendous effort, cleared the fence by the narrowest margin. But both front feet landed just in the ditch and he fell. It was a great weight of animal to fall, and Stephen was flung off him, clear off him, and landed with a heavy crunch among the rubble and stones.

Thereafter the world went black.

8

IT was on the Wednesday that Ross called on Dwight. It was the first showery day after a long fine spell, and the wind was getting up. Dwight was writing a letter to a Doctor Sutleffe, who had recently been called in to see if he could help the aged King. Dwight and Sutleffe had met in London and had kept up a sporadic correspondence. Sutleffe was prescribing a herbaceous tranquillizer, which he had found successful with many patients far gone in mania, but Dwight, though he did not say so in the letter, was not optimistic of its success when given to a blind man suffering from advanced dementia and now becoming deaf too. The only treatment Dwight would have prescribed was a far greater freedom for the harmless old King to move or be moved around his castle. He could do no damage to the realm.

When Ross was shown in Dwight got up, pen still in hand but smiling his welcome.

"I find you alone?" Ross said.

"Yes, they are all out — I believe on your beach. I think Caroline has gone rather against her will, as she is not fond of sandy feet. You're better?"

"Oh yes. Thank you. We both are. It's — something we shall learn to live with. Or live without."

115

"Demelza may be with Caroline. Have you come from the house? They are sure to have called."

"No, Demelza is away. She has gone to see Clowance. Troubles do not come singly. Stephen Carrington has met with a riding accident."

"I am very sorry. When did this happen?"

"Yesterday morning. He has recently bought a new horse and, it seems, was putting it through its paces when it fell at a fence and he with it. He was flung clear, but he has hurt his back, possibly broken it. At present he cannot move from the waist down."

Dwight made a face. "Where is he now?"

"At his house — his cottage. That is where Demelza has gone. Matthew Mark Martin has gone with her. They — "

"Was Clowance with him at the time?"

"No. Harriet was. I mean Harriet Warleggan. She fetched help from Cardew and he was carried home on a stretcher."

Dwight stroked his chin with the quill of his pen. "Who is attending him?"

"A man called Mather. Recently arrived from Bath. He did wonders for Andrew Blamey — old Andrew — when he was ill."

"Stephen may be better in a few days. Sometimes the shock paralyses as much as a real breakage . . . "

"But if it is a real breakage?"

"Can heal well enough in a few weeks or months. There is always the risk, of course."

"I'm sure."

"It depends very much where the injury is . . . Ill luck for him after such a triumphant voyage."

A shower of rain beat on the windows. Soon over, but it couldn't be the best day for a romp on the beach.

Ross said: "It does not seem so very long since Stephen was ill before, and you went across to advise and prescribe, and Clowance nursed him back to health."

"It *is* not so long."

Ross said: "Of course Clowance thinks there is only one doctor in Cornwall."

"I was afraid you might be intending to say that."

"I have the unenviable task of passing on her message to you. She said: 'Do please implore Uncle Dwight to come.'"

Dwight stroked his chin again.

"Of course I'll go. It is too late today, but perhaps tomorrow."

"Thank you. I know how grateful she would be."

"But I do not know how grateful this Dr Mather is likely to be! To preserve medical etiquette, it should be *he* who invites me to see his patient. Last time it was just an apothecary."

"If you were intending to go tomorrow, I would send someone over to tell them. I am sure that Clowance, helped by Demelza, would be able to convince any surgeon of the rightness of this course."

Dwight laughed. "I'll try to be there by eleven.

Mind you, Ross, in the case of an injury of the sort you describe — if it is such an injury, there's precious little anyone can do — surgeon or otherwise — except tell the patient to keep quiet and wait. Is he in much pain?"

"I don't know."

"Shall you be going to Penryn also?"

"I think not, at least until I have heard what you say. It is a small place and I don't want to overcrowd them. Also, Demelza must not be away too long."

"Oh?"

"Cuby is coming to stay."

★ ★ ★

When Dwight saw Ross out he saw Katie moving rapidly away among the trees of the drive, as if not wanting to be noticed. The shower had gone and Dwight was reluctant to return immediately to his letter, so he strolled towards the gates, enjoying the sun and the wind in his hair.

It occurred to him to think that perhaps Katie had brought another summons from Place House, but if that had been the case Bone would have come hurrying. In any event when he had last seen Selina she had seemed to have recovered her health and at least a degree of her spirits. Dwight guessed there had been a part reconciliation between husband and wife. However complex a character Valentine might be, and however mixed up in his own life, he had a great way with women, and there was

118

no reason to suppose that Selina had become immune.

Suddenly Katie was in front of him. She must have dodged round the corner of the drive, and it was as if she came upon him unexpectedly.

"Dr Enys . . . I was nearby and then I seen Cap'n Poldark."

"He's just gone," Dwight said. "Did you wish to see him?"

"Nay, twas you, sur, as I 'ad thoughts to see. But then I thought I'd no right nor reason to come'n bother ee."

"What is it? Are you unwell?"

"Nay, sur, I'm not unwell. Leastwise, not as no one could say so."

"I'm glad of that. What is it then?"

Katie's face was down, but he could see enough of it to observe the hot flush colouring all her visible skin.

"I don't hardly know 'ow to tell ee."

Dwight waited. "Would you like to come inside?"

"Oh, nay, sur, tedn that. But mebbe yes, maybe yes, I did oughter come in, not bawl'n out in the middle of the garden for everyone to 'ear."

"Good. Well, come in, then."

He led the way and she followed for a few paces and then stopped again. He waited.

She looked up and looped a tangle of hair away from one eye.

"I don't reckon tis proper, but maybe tis proper and right. I thinks only Surgeon d'know, so only he can tell me."

119

"Tell you what, Katie?"

She put a hand to her mouth as if willing herself not to speak.

"Reckon I've begun me courses again."

★ ★ ★

"Well, Katie," said Dwight, ten minutes later, "without a thorough examination, which I do not think you would wish to subject yourself to, I cannot tell what has been wrong with you. All I can say with certainty is that you are not going to have a baby."

"My dear life," she said, breathing out a sob. "I don't know how 't 'as 'appened!"

"Nor do I. But if what you now tell me is an exact description of what passed between yourself and Saul Grieves, I do not think you could possibly *be* pregnant. You see, merely the male seed . . . Well, there must be a much more definite penetration of the . . . Well, no matter. There are such things, you know, Katie, as false pregnancies. They can be brought on by hypnosis, hysteria, a wishful desire to have conceived, or a tremendous feeling of guilt. And the last is, I think, in your case the one to blame."

The intense flush was dying from Katie's sallow skin.

After a few moments she said: "What about this 'ere?" pointing to her swollen stomach.

"I shall expect it to go down naturally, now that you are convinced you have no child to bear. If it is a dropsical condition it can be treated. If tumorous it may be removable. But I am strongly of the opinion that in a healthy young woman such as yourself it is simply a symptom of hysteria and that it will very soon disappear."

Katie rubbed a hand across her eyes. "Jerusalem, it d'make me feel some queer, just to think on. All these months — months of sorrow and shame! They was all for naught."

"It should make your relief the greater."

"Oh, it do, it do. But I d'feel such a great lerrup. Gor 'elp me, what a great lerrup. Why . . . why I never needed tell nobody nothing! Nobody never needed to know I allowed Saul Grieves any liberties 'tall! Folk'll laugh me out of house an' home. Gor 'elp me. Tis enough to make you fetch up!"

"These things have happened before, Katie. There was a queen of England long ago called Mary who was just newly married and desperately wanted an heir to the throne. She convinced herself, and all the important Court doctors, that she was with child. Alas for her, she was not."

"She *wanted* a child," said Katie. "I *didn*!"

"It is probably derived from the mind in a similar way. I am sure your feelings of intense guilt — and your fear — produced the same symptoms."

There was the sound of horses outside. Caroline and the children had given up their trek on the beach. At the clatter Katie got up.

"Did she never have no children?"

"Who? The queen? No. Her sister inherited the throne."

"Well . . . that'll be your family come back from riding, Surgeon. I'll not keep ee no further. Tis for me to live my life — begin it all over afresh."

Dwight got up too. "Don't worry. Try not to be upset. It will be a nine-day wonder in the village and in no time at all everyone will forget it."

"My dear life!" Katie stopped as if she had been bitten.

"What is it?"

"Music!" said Katie, and slapped her thigh. "I shan't have to wed Music!"

There was a moment's pause before Dwight spoke. "No. You don't have to wed Music."

"My dear soul! Well, now, there's a relief for ee! Jer-us-alem! I don't have to wed no one 'tall!"

They went to the door.

"Music will be much upset."

"Ais, I s'pose. Do you think he 'ave ordinary feelings like a real man?"

"Emphatically so. Did you not realize that?"

"Ais, I s'pose. Ais, I d'know he be very fond of me. I like him too. There's no 'arm in him. Never a bad thought. 'E's gentle and kind. But I don't wish to wed 'im."

"Well," said Dwight dryly, "it is your own choice. It always has been."

There were more heavy clouds blowing up like angry fists clenched in the sky, but as she was let out of the side door, Katie squinted into a shaft of the expiring sun.

"I can't wed 'im *now*. Twas a convenience. Tis too bad for him maybe. I'm sorry for him, I really am. But there tis. He knew how twas. He'll 'ave to put up with un."

★ ★ ★

After leaving Dwight Ross took out the letter Cuby had written.

Dear Lady Poldark,

I am writing this from Caerhays where I have now been three weeks with my family. Perhaps I should first have written to you, but in truth it is hard to know what to say to the mother of the man I loved so dearly and who I know held him at least as dear. When we met last you were much concerned for the safety of Jeremy's father — and thank God he has come safe home — yet I remember it personally as a happy time when we first came to know each other and Jeremy was there to make our friendship complete. Now all is lost, and I propose to come to you carrying his child and carrying the grief of a bereavement we both equally share. Sir Ross told me I would be welcome at Nampara, to stay until after the birth of my child, and I feel sure that you would echo that welcome. But my constant presence in your household may come to be a too constant and irksome reminder of Jeremy's death, a lodestone dragging you ever back to your feeling of sorrow and loss.

So with your permission, dear Lady Poldark, I would like to come for perhaps two weeks, to begin, then perhaps to return to Caerhays for a little while. Let it be how it seems best and most seemly to you.

If it were convenient I would come next Monday, the 17th. I would like to bring my sister Clemency for company, who would stay the night and return with the groom on the following day. But pray make some other suggestion should this not be convenient. I am, as you well understand, entirely a free agent.

Believe me, dear Lady Poldark, I am so much looking forward to seeing you again.

Your loving daughter-in-law,
Cuby

Demelza had sent a note back saying she would be most welcome.

This was just before the young sailor had arrived to tell them of Stephen's accident.

★ ★ ★

In the afternoon Ross walked up to Wheal Grace, changed into mining things and went over it with Ben Carter. There was not much fresh to see, and what there was was depressing. For years the mine had yielded riches from several floors of tin and now was played out. The south floor had been closed for two years. The north, after appearing to be bottomed out more than once, had raised hopes by revealing smaller pockets and platforms from time to time, but none had more than postponed the evil day when the mine had to close.

While in captivity Ross had had plenty of time on his hands to make calculations, and he had come to the decision that if or when he got home the mine should be immediately shut down. By now there were only forty men working in it; all the others who had left had been absorbed into Wheal Leisure as that mine expanded. They could probably now take on another ten.

But Jeremy's death had knocked his calculations — like many other things — out of joint. He told Ben that for the time being the old mine should continue to operate but that the sixty-fathom level — the lowest there was — should be abandoned and such work as there was could be concentrated on the forty-fathom and above. The bottom pumps — installed by Jeremy — were to be disconnected and brought up — and anything else of value before the old floors were submerged. Beth, the engine built by Bull & Trevithick twenty-five years ago, and modernized by Jeremy in 1811, could continue to function on a reduced scale and under reduced stress. Labour force could be pared down to about thirty. It was more than maintenance, but not a lot. It would cut his profits on Wheal Leisure by about twenty per cent.

Ben asked if he would go over Leisure with him tomorrow, but Ross said it would have to be one day next week. There was no reason for this — he was not busy — except that Leisure in the last five years had become so much Jeremy's mine (the whole decision to reopen it, the design of the engine, the leats to bring the fresh water, the development of the rediscovered Trevorgie workings) that he just did not wish to face it again. He had made a perfunctory tour when he first came home, but then the wound had still been so raw that it couldn't be made worse.

It was only about four and a half years ago, just after he had returned from Spain — and they had been down Wheal Grace and were walking back to the house together — that Jeremy had made the suggestion that they might consider reopening Wheal Leisure. He had interlaced his remarks with seemingly innocent queries about the Trevanions — apparently he had just then met the girl for the first time and was besotted with her. Ross knew nothing of this then — Cuby and Jeremy had first met when Jeremy was returning from some adventure he had undertaken with Stephen Carrington and they had come ashore near Caerhays. An ill-fated affair if ever there was one; yet it seemed to have contained within it a short vivid few months of brilliant happiness. Perhaps that was better than nothing at all. And Cuby, although in some ways wilful and perverse, had been a girl worthy of his love.

The other thing Ross had not known that chilly morning in February 1811 was Jeremy's intense preoccupation with the development of steam — and the gift that he had for harnessing the latest ideas. Ross never failed to blame himself for this lack of knowledge, this lack of

126

perception in regard to his son. Yet, as Demelza had said, Jeremy had preserved such secrecy about it that there was no *way* of knowing. It had, as so often happened between father and son, been a breakdown in communication rather than a breakdown in sympathy.

And then, before he died, so very young, he had even begun to distinguish himself in a military career, picked out by Wellington himself for promotion. Another Captain Poldark. Somehow the art of war was the last thing one would have ever expected him to excel at, the tall, thin, gangling, artistic young man with the slight stoop, the joking, flippant manner, the distaste for bloodshed.

God, Ross thought, what a *waste*! what a *loss*! — for Demelza, for Cuby, for Isabella-Rose, above all for Jeremy himself . . .

He was about to leave the shelter of the mine when his temporarily blurred sight picked out the figure of another young man approaching. As tall as Jeremy, younger by three years, long-nosed and narrow-eyed and thin-shanked, dark of hair and skin, a lock showing over his brow from under his hat. His cloak and features were glistening from the latest shower.

"Well, Cousin Ross or I'll be damned! What nasty weather! Were you in the mine? Good fortune for you. I wasn't, as you observe. These clouds just dip the water out of the sea and empty it like a child with a bucket!"

His glinting, easy, charming smile. But just the wrong moment for Ross, remembering Jeremy.

"I thought you were back in Oxford."

"Cambridge. No, we leave at the weekend. Ghastly journey, but Selina will not go by sea. A pertinent disadvantage to making one's home in Cornwall is the monstrous distance it is from everywhere else!" He got off his horse, glancing at Ross's gaunt, grim face. "We wrote, of course, as soon as we heard."

"Of course," said Ross. "Thank you. I'm sure Demelza replied."

"I believe Clowance did. It is a sad loss for us all."

"Thank you."

Valentine had dismounted. Ross noticed the slightly bent leg.

"Are you walking back?"

"Yes. But I have to warn you, Demelza is from home. She is staying with Clowance for a few days."

"It was about Clowance that I was come to ask. Or if not Clowance, then Stephen. I have heard he has had an accident."

"Bad news travels fast." As they began to walk downhill Ross told the young man what he knew.

Valentine said: "That is cursed luck. I have come to know Stephen over the last couple of years and find him an energetic, versatile feller. He will not take kindly to a long spell of invalidism."

"Dr Enys is going tomorrow, so perhaps we shall have more information then."

The small angry clouds marching in from the north-west had separated, like a military procession before an obstacle, and between them the sky above Nampara had become sea-green and shot through with sunshine. Valentine took off his hat and flapped it against his cloak, knocking away the moisture. He asked about the progress of Wheal Leisure and Wheal Grace, and spoke of his own new venture, Wheal Elizabeth, which by the beginning of next year was likely to need an engine.

"I had been going to seek Jeremy's advice on this. Alas . . . "

"When shall you get your degree?"

"Next spring. We hope to be permanently in residence at Place House from then on. May I ask you one or two questions?"

A change of tone.

"Questions? Of course. If I can answer them. Will you come in?"

"Let us walk down to the beach. Maybe the open air will be better for any confidences which may pass."

They skirted Demelza's garden and came out on the rough ground leading to Nampara Beach, where the mallows and the thistles and the rough grass grew. The tide was out, and the expanse of sand stretched to the Dark Cliffs, smooth, pale brown, uninterrupted by rock or shelf or gully. The sand nearby was well pitted with footprints, but beyond a few hundred yards even they disappeared. In the distance a solitary figure moved along the high-water mark.

"Paul Daniel," said Ross.

"What?"

"Paul Daniel. He shares this part of the beach with three others who go up and down the

129

high-water mark seeing what's come in. When he finds something on the way out he does not pick it up but makes a double cross beside it in the sand. Woe betide anyone who makes off with it."

Valentine laughed. "We are both Cornish to the bone, you and I, Cousin Ross; yet I suspect you understand the villagers far better than I ever shall."

"My early life was more earthy. Certainly until I left to go overseas in my early twenties I had never been further than Plymouth."

" . . . I have been away so much."

They leaned on the gate.

"What did you wish to ask me?"

The breeze was not interrupted for some time.

"You mentioned Dwight Enys just now. He attended my mother when my sister was born."

"I believe so."

"Did he attend her when I was born?"

"No, he was at sea — in the navy."

"You know I was an eight-month child?"

"I have heard so."

"Premature in all things. But you say you have *heard* so. Did you not know so, as you lived so near by?"

"My relationship with the Warleggan family has never been friendly. At that time it was at its worst."

"Why?"

"Why what?"

"Why was it so bad just then?"

"Is this an examination I have to face?"

"If you please."

Valentine was tapping on the gate with his long fingers. This young man had been a figure in Ross's thoughts, frequently forgotten and then painfully, poignantly central again, for more than twenty years. Yet in all that time they had never had a personal, intimate discussion. Their contact had been superficial. It seemed peculiarly maladroit that Elizabeth's son should tackle him in this way so soon after Jeremy's death. He had always tended to dislike the young man, his sardonic humour, his mischievous jokes, his great charm, his automatic assumption that all women would succumb to it. He had been particularly disagreeable at Geoffrey Charles's party, had brought Conan Whitworth uninvited and greatly upset Morwenna, had half-drunkenly smiled and sneered through the tense encounter following, when Ross and George had almost come to blows again. Rumour had it that he had married Selina Pope for her money and was already being openly unfaithful to her.

"What are you looking at?" Valentine asked.

"At you, Valentine, since you ask. At the time you were born, the natural antagonism between me and your father was at its height because I had not wished your mother to marry him. He must have known this."

"You were in love with my mother, were you not?"

"At one time."

"At that time?"

"I held her in high esteem."

Ross watched a parade of crows which were

waddling in judicial procession towards the cliffs of Wheal Leisure as if about to open the assizes.

Valentine said: "Did you know — I suspect you did — that I was a constant bone of contention between my mother and father?"

"Later, yes."

"So you must have known why." When Ross did not answer Valentine said: "Because he suspected I was not his son."

"Indeed?"

"Yes, indeed. All my childhood I lived under this cloud, though of course I did not know what it then was. After my mother died it lifted a lot. It was as if Ursula's birth — at seven months — had allayed his suspicions. After that he made an effort in his own dry dusty way to become an agreeable father. But by then the damage — so far as I was concerned — was done. I feared him and hated him. There was little he could do by then to change himself in my eyes. I . . . I have always felt he was in some way responsible for my mother's death."

"I do not think that could be. Your — George — was very attached to your mother; no doubt, as you say, in his own dry dusty way; but I believe it to have been genuine. Do not forget that it was twelve years before he remarried."

Paul Daniel had moved out of sight. Ross felt a surge of fruitless anger at the tangle of love and hate and jealousy which had surrounded this young man's birth and distorted his childhood. Whose fault was it? His as much as anyone's. Elizabeth's too. And

132

George's. The one blameless person was surely Valentine. Through the years, and always at a distance, Ross had watched the boy's progress to manhood. Yes, what he had seen and heard had been unfavourable. But too seldom had he faced the facts of his own responsibility, psychological or actual, for the situation as it had come about.

This unsought meeting stung him emotionally, made him feel as if the central fact of his whole existence, the hub from which all the spokes of his later experience led away, lay in the few minutes of anger and lust and overpowering frustration from which Valentine could have been born.

He put his hand on Valentine's arm, briefly. It was an uncharacteristic gesture.

"Why have you come to see me today?"

"I felt that before I left again I had to meet you, try to straighten out certain events in my own mind."

"I do not think I can help."

"That was what Dwight Enys said when I spoke to him a few days ago."

"On this subject?"

"Related to this subject . . . Do you think my mother was unfaithful to George Warleggan after they were married?"

"Good God, no! You demean her memory."

"I cannot help but speculate. It would explain his extraordinary changes of mood."

"I'm sure that is not the explanation."

"Do you then feel equally certain that my mother went with no man between the time

133

her first husband died and the day of her remarriage?"

Ross had seen this question coming. "Your mother was an upright and honourable woman. I saw little of her, but I should think it highly unlikely."

Valentine coughed dryly. "Well, may I ask a final question, then. It is the one I came to ask, difficult as it may be to ask it. Is it possible that you could be my father?"

Ross found he was gripping the top of the gate too tightly. He slackened the grip and then flexed his fingers, looking at them. He knew how much might depend on his reply. And how necessary it was *instantly* to lie, without the *least* hesitation. Instantly. And yet how *impossible* it was to lie whatever the consequences.

"I have no intention of answering your question, Valentine."

"You mean you can't or won't?"

"Both."

Wheal Leisure was coaling. Black smoke rose and merged with the cloud drifting above it and began its journey of dispersal inland.

Valentine said: "Then it is a possibility?"

"God damn you, boy!" Ross stopped and swallowed, trying to contain his anger, aware that it was as much directed at himself as at his questioner. There was silence for a few moments. "Damn you! . . . Yes, it is a possibility." As Valentine was about to speak Ross went savagely on: "But *only* a possibility. No one will ever know for certain. I do not think your mother ever knew for certain. It is

134

a question that I cannot answer for I do not know the answer. Does that satisfy you?"

Valentine said thoughtfully: "Yes, thank you. I think it does."

It seemed as if, because of what had happened that moment, the world was moving in a different way, as if a few words uttered into the wind, spoken by a single voice, heard by one person alone, would prevent its ever being the same place again.

Ross said: "But let me warn you. Let me warn you of this, Valentine. If at any time you speak of this — in public or in private, claiming something or denying something on the strength of what I have said, there will be two men wanting to kill you. That is George Warleggan and myself. And I swear to you one of us will."

Valentine leaned back against the gate in his usual cynical attitude, as if nothing was more important than that he should seem to care about nothing in the world. But his face was deeply flushed. Returning the gesture, he put a hand on Ross's arm.

"Understood," he said, "Cousin Ross."

9

WHEN Dwight reached Penryn the following morning Clowance opened the door and showed him into the tiny parlour, where a thick-set blond boy was standing hands in pockets.

"This is Jason Carrington, Stephen's nephew. He has just called to see Stephen."

They shook hands. Clowance was rather untidy, her eyes bloodshot from lack of sleep.

After an awkward moment Jason said: "Well, ma'am. I reckon I'd best be getting back. I'll be here tomorrow for sure."

When he had gone Dwight said: "I can see the relationship."

"Yes . . . He is very fond of Stephen."

"Tell me how it all happened."

"He was thrown from his horse in the woods below Cardew. Lady Harriet was with him. According to the groom they had not met above fifteen minutes before and were galloping towards Cardew. They came to an awkward fence and Stephen's horse fell. Harriet went for help and he was put in a farm cart so that he could lie flat and be brought home. Even though the distance was much greater than Cardew, they considered it better to bring him straight here." Dwight thought there was a touch of bitterness in her tone.

"And now? He is conscious?"

"Oh yes. Has been since Thursday. But sometimes confused still."

"Can he move his legs?"

"He can move his left but not his right. Dr Mather has put him in what he calls a spinal jacket and has bled him constantly. Mama is with him at the moment."

"And Dr Mather knows I am coming?"

"We told him this morning. Of course he knows your name. He said he would try to be back by eleven, so that you can see Stephen together."

Dwight took out his watch. It was only 10.15. "Does Dr Mather live near? Perhaps I could call on him."

"At Flushing. I suppose it's three or four miles."

There was a step outside and Demelza came in. She was wearing a white muslin frock with a black sash, and Dwight thought her looks were already a little returning, almost in spite of herself.

They kissed. Demelza said: "He is thirsty, and I came down for more lemonade. Tis that good of you to come, Dwight. Caroline did not ride with you?"

"No. She thought it would make a crowd."

After talking for a few minutes it was Demelza who said: "Dr Mather is an understanding physician. I do not believe he can be too put about if you go up without him."

Stephen looked a big man lying in the small trestle bed, much bigger than when Dwight had attended him for the peripneumonia. His face was heavy and flushed. Demelza put the lemonade on a side-table and said: "I will wait downstairs."

Stephen's body was bound up in splints, and he grunted as they turned him over on his side. Dwight's fingers travelled lightly over his back, pressing to see where there was pain. The right leg was swollen and useless, the skin dark and bruised-looking. The left leg he could bring up to bend his knee.

They turned him again on his back, and Clowance propped him up a few inches with a couple of pillows.

Dwight took out a glass tube with a small bulb at one end, attached to a thin cane rod for strength. He put this under Stephen's arm. The clinical thermometer had been invented nearly two decades ago but was not in general use. When he withdrew it he saw the mercury well up the scale.

"I'm steering a fair course," Stephen said. "Full canvas soon. Rest for a day or two more. That's all. Gi' me the lemonade, Clowance."

He could hold the glass but his hands were shaky. Dwight lifted his eyelids.

"You should mend," he said, "but it will be a slow process. You will need to possess patience. Dr Mather is following the right treatment." He said to Clowance: "I think the bruising on the right leg would be reduced with a liniment of camphor dissolved in oil of cloves. But do not cover with a flannel cloth, allow the air to reach it. And I will write a prescription for Peruvian bark. Then I must see Dr Mather."

138

"They sent up from the Royal Standard last night," Stephen said, "wishing me well. Eh? And Christopher Saverland, the Packet agent, sent his wishes. And others've called. It just shows."

There were adverse signs here and Dwight wondered whether Mather had been alert to them — and if he had whether he had kept them to himself.

"There's some spinal damage," he said as they went down the stairs, "but the recovery of movement in the left leg is a good sign. The oedematous condition of the right leg will have to be watched. I believe bleeding will serve a useful purpose, though at the base of the spine, not on the leg itself."

"How long will he be bedridden?" Clowance asked.

"It is impossible to know, my dear. Three months, if he is fortunate."

"Three months!"

"It may be less. He is a very determined man. But first . . . "

"First?" said Demelza, studying the face of her old friend.

"Can he eat? He should be kept on an antiphlogistic regime. Lemonade is the ideal drink."

"First?" said Demelza.

"There has been some internal bleeding. It may have already stopped."

"And if it has not?"

"Let us hope it has. When are you returning home?"

"Me?" said Demelza. "I don't know for

certain sure. But I have to go Monday."

"I think Mama should return home soon in any case," said Clowance. "She has enough troubles of her own without bearing mine. And Jeremy's widow is coming to Nampara to stay."

"Can you manage him on his own?"

"Jason will be here Monday to stay as long as I need him. He can help me with any of the heavy work of nursing."

"After I have seen Dr Mather," Dwight said, "perhaps I might come back and take a bite to eat with you before setting off home?"

* * *

Aristide Mather said: "There is a definite fracture of the vertebrae. Palsy was total when I saw him first. I made an incision yesterday in the right thigh and drew a quantity of blood."

"Yes, I saw that."

"The swelling was reduced and he seemed eased by it. I also raised the sacrum by means of a levator. That too you will have observed."

"Did it cause him great pain?"

"He grunted a deal. He is not one, I think, over-sensitive to pain."

"The right thigh is the greatest concern," Dwight said.

"Internal haemorrhaging?"

"Yes."

"I thought of the femoral artery."

"So did I. But if it had been ruptured he would have been dead by now . . . "

140

"Well, there's little we can do for that. There is no way of applying a tourniquet."

Mather was about forty, short, brisk, red haired, with that capable confident air Dwight had always lacked.

"I should like to see him again, perhaps in a couple of days, if that would be agreeable to you."

"Perfectly. Pray come when you wish."

"Lady Poldark will, I think, be riding home on Monday. If you would send word by her — in a letter, I mean — that would keep me informed."

"Certainly. If he is still alive by then."

Dwight raised his eyebrows.

"Well every day is a day gained," he said drily.

As they reached the door Mather said: "I read your article on malign and benign growths and the tubercles of phthisis in the *Edinburgh Medical & Surgical Journal*. I am honoured to meet the author."

"Ah," said Dwight, almost apologetically. "That was last year. I have recently come upon one or two new points, which might slightly amend the argument. But thank you."

"In the meantime rest assured I shall do all I can to bring this young friend of yours to a recovery. I have always found it as well to fear the worst — in my own mind — so that I am fully prepared to fight it."

"It is a principle I follow myself," said Dwight. "So I am not likely to quarrel with it. I shall await your letter, Dr Mather."

When he got home it was after six and Music had been waiting for him three hours.

Dwight had eaten well at Clowance's, so, having satisfied Caroline's inquiries about Stephen, he was able to delay her thoughts on food until he had seen the young man.

Music said: "Tedn right fur me to bother ee, Surgeon, but her said yes, Surgeon, her promised me. Her promised."

He had been crying, but that was a time ago. His light eyes, in which intelligence had only its intermittent leasehold, were dry enough now, prominent, but for him quite hard. He kept swallowing his Adam's apple as if he were trying to get rid of it.

"I'm sorry for you, Music. There is little I can do to help."

"I d'know that. Thur be nothink nobody can do. But what can *I* do, Surgeon? It d'leave me out of the cold. Worked every hour on that thur cottage. She've been over him wi' me time an' time. Tedn as if I'd *changed*. Bain't no change in me. I 'aven't gone moonstruck nor mops an' brooms, nor nothink. She've just broke 'er promise, that be the whole truth of it!"

Dwight said: "You realize, I'm sure, that she believed herself to be pregnant and was going to marry you partly for the sake of the child. When it turned out all to be a mistake, the main reason for the marriage had been removed."

"Please?"

"She is a virgin, Music, if you know what that

142

means. She has never had proper intercourse with a man. She finds herself a girl again. Life for her is beginning afresh. She has total freedom of choice and at present prefers to choose no one — to be what she was before all this began, Katie Carter, a parlourmaid at Place House."

"Please?"

Dwight's mouth turned in a grim smile. "Come, my friend, do not step back so quickly. But do not think I don't sympathize with you. She agreed to marry you and — "

"Twas a promise!"

"Yes, it was, and she has broken it, and she should not have done. But she thinks everything has changed and that that releases her from her undertaking. I suppose she explained this to you?"

"She said this an' that. This an' that."

"And did she not say she was sorry?"

"Oh aye. She said she was some sorry and tried to pertend we'd be friends. But that bain't the same thing 'tall."

"I know. I know how disappointed you must be. And since I encouraged the match I must bear some responsibility. I am very sorry and disappointed this has happened. It is a lesson to me not to interfere in other people's lives."

"Please?"

"But, Music, you must not allow this to be an excuse for backsliding. You came to me for advice and help long before your involvement with Katie — or at least long before it became serious. And I *have* helped and advised you, haven't I?"

Music scratched his head. " . . . Ais."

"So there is no excuse to allow all that to slip away again. You must *not* let your disappointment get the better of you and so return to become the young man you were three years ago. You are so much better. You are normal in nearly every way. You must remain so — even if it means leaving Place House and never seeing Katie again. You must be your own man. Understand?"

"Ais."

"Now go home and tell yourself you are going to make the best of it. Will you promise me?"

With a large slack hand Music pushed the lank hair out of his eyes.

"Cann't promise to leave Place House."

"I don't ask that. I only suggest it as a last resort. Promise you will keep up your present efforts to be a whole man."

Music blinked. "I *be* a whole man, Surgeon. That d'bring me no comfort."

★ ★ ★

When she rode home on Monday there was a conflict in Demelza's mind. The black gaping hole of Jeremy's death was still there in the very depths of her body, like a canker that ate away any sign of a return of her natural high-spirited interest in life as soon as it stirred in her. She was much concerned about Stephen who, if no worse, was certainly no better, and she carried Dr Mather's letter for Dr Enys and was tempted to open it and see what his real opinion was.

144

But aside from these troubles was an altogether less worthy worry, which she knew Ross would despise her for. Her daughter-in-law was coming to stay.

And bringing her sister, whom she had scarcely met.

The two weeks in Brussels, where Cuby and Jeremy had made her and the other three so very welcome, had passed off beautifully, and if it had not been for her worry about Ross — when in the last six months had she ever been free from worry? — she would have enjoyed herself. The very first time she had met Cuby — only last year — she had felt a certain affinity with and liking for the girl. This had been much enhanced in Brussels, and she had looked forward to seeing more of her whenever she could. After the loss of Jeremy she had fully endorsed Ross's suggestion that Cuby should come to live at Nampara at least until the baby was born.

But now that it came to the point, old feelings related to her humble birth stirred in her.

Cuby had never been to Nampara, which, to face the truth, was only a large farmhouse with a fair range of outbuildings common to a farm, and only one room really, the library, to give it the claim to be called something better. Nampara Manor? It wouldn't do. It wouldn't be true. You don't elevate a thing by giving it a better name.

She had never been to Caerhays, not even to see it from the outside; but Jeremy had spoken of it quite often — a great castle (even if an imitation one which they had not yet been

145

able to afford to finish), set in a superb park, with footmen and grooms and all the panoply of aristocratic living. Demelza knew such houses. She knew them well. Tehidy, Tregothnan, Trelissick. She loved them and enjoyed the company of the people living in them. Bowood, where she had taken Clowance, was the greatest of them all. And she had stayed in Lansdowne House only a few weeks ago. She had mixed with the best. And she was now Lady Poldark.

So why this worry? Well, Cuby had never seen Nampara. It was an earthy place, with a down-to-earth master and an up-from-the-mines mistress. Cuby had been over last year to the party at Trenwith. Now *that* was a suitable house, belonging to Geoffrey Charles. Perhaps Cuby expected Nampara to be another Trenwith. If so, it would be a horrid come-down for her. It seemed that she had become reconciled with her family. Probably after a couple of weeks she would gratefully return to Caerhays and stay there. Even though her mother-in-law was Lady Poldark.

And there was a sister coming. Demelza had seen her at the Trenwith party, along with a rather bumptious brother (with whom Cuby had recently been staying in London). Demelza seemed to remember that Jeremy had spoken well of the sister, though whether this was the same one remained to be seen.

With Jeremy none of this would have mattered. He would have jollied everything along, filled up the awkward pauses, adorned

146

the house, in Cuby's eyes, with his presence. Now there was only Ross, who in his existing mood was more than ever inclined to disregard the niceties.

So she left Penryn very early on Monday, accompanied by the same young sailor who had brought the last message, and was home by eleven. In her reply to Cuby she had invited them to dinner at three, and now wished she had not. There was little enough time to prepare, first, two bedrooms, and then a meal which, while not pretentious, must be pleasantly elegant and well chosen.

All this, as she had instructed before she left, was in train, but much needed still to be done. The parlour was untidy, the dining-room cheerless, the *washing* had to be taken in; and the whole house lacked flowers. To make matters worse a strong south-easterly wind was blowing — always the most difficult to cope with — making windows rattle and doors bang. The tallest sandhills beyond Wheal Leisure were smoking as if they had volcanic properties.

She flew about the house, even making a heart-hurting tidy up of Jeremy's bedroom, so that if Cuby wanted to see it it should look its best. She had given Clemency Clowance's room and Cuby the better of the two new rooms built above the library when that part of the house was altered in '96. This, if she eventually chose to stay, would be where she would bear her baby. It was the least used room in the house and quite the most genteel. Only five years ago they had bought new rosewood furniture, the bed

147

had pink quilted satin hangings and furnishings, with window curtains to match, and there was a maroon turkey carpet.

Into the garden to gather flowers; but they were sparse and looked tired. Cornish gardens were at their best in the spring: the light warm soil favoured all kinds of bulbs, roses, broom, lupins, wallflowers and flowering shrubs like lilac and veronica. But there was not enough humus to sustain the summer and autumn flowers at their best. (This year, of course, the hollyhocks had quite failed.) Dahlias were becoming all the rage and might have done well in this sandy soil, but Demelza could never grow them because of memories of Monk Adderley.

She had gathered what to her looked a tattered bunch, had thrust them into a jug in the parlour, and hastened out to see if she could find something more, when Ross came into the garden by the gate leading to the sea.

"Back so soon?" he said as he kissed her. "I had not expected you till twelve."

She told him between stoopings and snippings the latest news on Stephen.

"I brought a note for Dwight from Dr Mather. I had no time to deliver it on the way home, and I did not like to trust it with the sailor. Perhaps Matthew Mark would take it."

"I can take it myself."

"No, Ross, if you please, I would rather you were here when Cuby comes."

He took her arm. "It is not the old bogeys rising again?"

"A small matter maybe. But I have never had

a daughter-in-law before, and because of what has happened it is bound to be difficult." She gazed round disparagingly at her garden. "If I had time I could do better with the wild flowers on the cliffs! There's heather in plenty, and knapweed — and there's lovely fresh gorse at the top of the Long Field."

"Well, it will take you no more than half an hour. I'll hold the fort while you are gone."

Demelza shook her head. Sick fancies these days: she had a sudden vivid picture of coming into this house, before she married Ross, a servant girl carrying a sheaf of bluebells, and finding Elizabeth had called.

"Why are you shivering?" Ross asked.

"Was I? It is of no moment . . . I think Stephen is gravely ill, Ross. I wish I knew what Dr Mather had written to Dwight."

"I will go myself tonight and ask him. He'll tell me. But in injuries like this the surgeons can do little. It all depends on the patient and how bad he is hurt."

"My dear life!" said Demelza.

"What is it?"

"I think they are here."

★ ★ ★

"He don't seem to get rid of the fever," said Jason.

"No. I hope Dr Enys will come again soon."

"Reckon he did no more than Surgeon Mather."

"It is just that I have known him so long and

trust his judgements. I had hoped . . . "

They were eating some fried soles that Jason had bought, with potatoes and a pease pudding. Clowance had listlessly prepared the meal and ate without appetite. It was the evening of the Tuesday, still light because the sun, though setting over the land, reflected an incandescence from the water of the bay. Dr Mather had been in this afternoon and given the patient a draught which had put him to sleep, and had left another for the night. They were taking it in turns to be with him and had put up another trestle bed in the room so that each in turn could spend the night there. Stephen was in some pain now, but he was too weak to be irritable. All the same his weakness had not prevented him spending a part of the morning planning with Jason the boat that he intended to buy or have built, a smallish brig or a twenty-five-foot lugger, for Jason to command until he was experienced enough to merit something bigger.

Nor had it prevented him seeing three visitors: Andrew Blamey, Sid Bunt and Timothy Hodge. The first had been just a friendly call, a hail and farewell, for Andrew was sailing for New York on the morning tide and came to wish him well. The last two had been on business, for trade had to continue even with the owner laid up.

Clowance had hardly spoken with Tim Hodge before: he was so swart, so dark of eye and skin and tooth, so squat, that it took a time to overlook his appearance; then you couldn't fail to appreciate his practical talents. If Stephen was to be laid up for a long time he was the obvious man to help to run things. If she had not been so preoccupied with Stephen she might have had time to wonder how a man of such parts, now in his mid-forties, should still have had to enrol as an ordinary deckhand in a makeshift privateering venture.

Jason said: "Father's a real popular man. Folk stop me in the street, say, how is he, seem real concerned."

"He has a way with him," said Clowance. "He gets on well with everyone."

She looked across the table at Jason, whose appetite was good and who ate with a relish worthy of a starving sailor. Since Stephen's accident she had seen a lot more of his son. He seemed the natural person to help her at a time like this. She saw in him some of Stephen's traits, both unagreeable and endearing, particularly among the former his tendency to fantasize on his own prospects, his ability in his own mind to rearrange the world to his own wishes. He would never be as good-looking as Stephen, nor, she thought, as physically, so vitally, attractive; but he had an engaging manner, an optimism, a resilience that reminded her very much of the man upstairs.

Thinking these things, Clowance said to him: "Tell me about your mother."

Jason blinked, then smiled. "What do ye wish to know, ma'am?"

"Well, do you think you are like her?"

"Nay, she were dark and thin — real thin in later years — and small-boned — like a quail. I've taken from my father."

151

"You are not quite as big as he is. Did she have any special abilities?"

"Abilities?"

"Well, I mean, was she, for instance, a good cook? I'm not a very good cook."

"Good 'nough, ma'am. I'm sure my father love the food you give him. Mother? Yes, she did for us well. How my father liked it I don't know, because, of course, he left."

"Yes, he left."

Jason took a draught of ale. "She was a good sewer."

"Knitting and weaving?"

"Knitting special. She helped bring me up wi' selling things she made wi' her own hands. This jerkin, f'instance."

Clowance looked at it and smiled. "It was the one good thing you were wearing when you came. The stitch is very even."

"Well, she made it for me. She made many things for me — stockings, gloves. This jerkin was one of the last things she made for me, more'n two years ago."

Clowance put a piece of bread in her mouth. It was home-made and light, but it lacked something. Perhaps it was salt. She cut another slice from the loaf.

"Two years ago?"

There was a silence.

Jason said: "Hark, was that him tapping? I thought I heard — "

"No, I don't think so . . . Did you say your mother knitted this for you two years ago?"

"Oh, nay, twas a slip of the tongue. Twas

152

much longer than two year." Jason had gone very red.

"How much longer?" Clowance asked.

"I think I'll go see if he is awake," Jason said, pushing back his chair. "I wouldn't wish for him to think he was alone."

He went out, and Clowance cut the piece of bread into small cubes. But they still tasted ashen and saltless.

After a while Jason came back. "No, he's fast asleep still, but I have lit a candle. The light is failing, and when he wakes it will be good to see a light."

"Jason," Clowance said. "When did your mother die?"

"What?" He blinked. His eyes were smaller than Stephen's, sandy lashed.

"She isn't still alive, is she?"

"Who? My mother? God's sake, no, she died — oh, some long time ago."

"When?"

He scratched his head and then took an uncomfortable swig of beer. "I don't rightly remember."

"You don't *remember* when your *mother* died? Oh, Jason, I don't believe that! Did your father tell you to lie to me?"

"Oh, nay! But he just said — well, not to talk about her — said it would be like to upset ye."

Without getting up, Clowance began to tidy the table, putting plates together and gathering spoons. She was doing it instinctively, with no awareness of her actions.

153

"Well, it does," she said. "It does upset me a little to hear your mother died so recent. But now I am upset, I think I would like to know the whole of it."

"Twas a fool thing!" said Jason. "A damn fool thing to let it out wi' a slip of the tongue! Twould distress Father greatly to think I had been gossiping behind his back, like."

"You are not gossiping. And I will not tell your father. Was it last December she died?"

"God's sake, no! Long afore that."

"I thought perhaps as soon as your mother died you came to tell your father, and so turned up here last January?"

"Nay, nay, she died in the winter."

"Last winter?"

"Nay."

"The winter before? You may as well tell me, as I can easy find out." (She did not know how, but it was a point to make.)

"The winter before," said Jason. "I remember snow was on the ground. Twould be in the January."

"January 1814?"

"Yes . . . "

"Two years ago your father went back to Bristol for a time. Five years ago he *came* from Bristol here for the first time. Was your father living with your mother, or visiting her there?"

"Lord no, we never seen him! I'd never seen him, not for twelve or more year before I came here this January, and that's God's truth! We didn't live in Bristol but ten mile outside. We never heard tell of him until I heard of him

154

at Christmas time, last Christmas time. Then a man, a Cornish sailor called Tregellas, he said he knew my father was newly wed and living in Penryn and was well found with a fleet of ships. So I thought to come, and come I did, as you well know."

Clowance got up now, carried the plates across to the scullery.

When she came back she said: "Did your father know of your mother's death?"

Jason looked startled. "Oh, yes! Oh yes! Well he must've, mustn't he. Before he could wed you."

10

THE arrival had gone off quite well, and five of them sat down to dinner: Cuby and Clemency, Ross and Demelza and Isabella-Rose. Henry, who usually ate the main afternoon meal with them, was taking it with Mrs Kemp in the kitchen.

In spite of her pallor Cuby looked well. She showed the coming child more obviously than a taller lady on the south coast, who was about as much forward; but like Harriet pregnancy was doing no hurt to her looks. Nor did her bereavement show. Possibly it was the effect of coming to see her late husband's family in their home for the first time that made her vivacious and talkative — much more so than her quieter, plainer, gentler sister. From her green riding costume she had changed into a plain dress of blue dimity, with blue and white ribbons, velvet shoes. No mourning except for a small posy of black artificial flowers pinned to her breast. She had changed her hairstyle, Demelza noticed, grown it, wore it in bracelets of braided hair. Her rather sulky face lit up when she smiled: good brilliant teeth, warm lips.

They were eating hare soup, a green goose, pickled salmon, cheese cake, almond cream, with cider and beer. It was not elegant enough, Demelza thought, but Ross had said it was right.

Cuby said on the way over she had noticed the barley and wheat had been cut but most of the oats were still standing. The ground had been very wet, Ross said; this wind would soon dry it. He supposed crops were a week or two ahead on the more sheltered south coast? Cuby spoke about the excellent carriageway that had been laid between Truro and Shortlanesend, she swore it was the best in Cornwall. Ross said, yes, yes, it was the work of that man from Ayrshire, MacArthur, or MacAdam, was it? Clemency asked about a mine they had passed near Truro, and Ross said, oh that would be Guarnek, re-started last year; it was said to be doing well. Cuby said, was this your mine, the engine that was working as they came down the valley? Yes, said Ross, industry passes too close here to achieve elegance . . . Cuby said she was sure everyone would welcome some industry close to Caerhays if it would contribute to their income.

"In fact," said Ross, "the mine you passed, though it has made us a small fortune over the years, is now costing us money to maintain. At one time we employed more than a hundred and forty people, now it is down to thirty. Wheal Leisure, over on the cliff, is the profitable one."

"But you keep this other, this . . . "

"Wheal Grace. Just in operation. It is partly sentiment, partly that I don't want to throw men out of work. While I was interned I thought it over and decided it must close. But coming home, with later events in mind, I have kept it

157

open. I think Jeremy would have wanted it kept open."

The name was out. No one spoke for a few moments. Knives and forks chattered instead.

Cuby said: "Lady Poldark, did you hear that Lady Fitzroy Somerset had her baby in Brussels? In May. It was a girl, but I do not know how she has been named."

"No," said Demelza. "After I left Brussels I did not see her again."

Ross said: "I'm told Fitzroy will continue in the army and a brilliant future is foretold for him. He seems completely to have overcome the loss of an arm. The Falmouths say he is in fine fettle."

"It is not so bad as losing a leg," said Isabella-Rose brightly. "Though it may be worse, I dare suppose, than losing only a foot."

They all looked at this inconsequence in slight surprise, but she was not abashed. "Do you know what happened yesterday, Cuby? A kite was hovering over the chicken run, quite close, when Ena — one of our maids — rushed out to save the chick. The kite came down and stuck its claws in her cap and carried it off! It was so comical! We was convulsed with laughter."

You used always, Demelza thought, to be able to rely on Bella to keep the conversation going on a jolly note; but since learning of Jeremy's death and Christopher Havergal's maiming she had been very mopish; often over a meal she hardly uttered a word; so it was a startling and welcome surprise to find her with recovered spirits at such an opportune time.

Now she was asking if Cuby sang, saying that Jeremy had told her she did — using the name without embarrassment — and that Clemency played; so tomorrow they must try duets together before Clemency left; they had a lovely piano — not that old spinet — but a lovely new one in the library that Papa had bought a couple of years ago; and no doubt they would be given permission to play on it for such a special guest.

Demelza went on with her dinner, picking at this and that, and noticing that Cuby was not eating heartily either, but watching her lips part in a smile, those crescent dimples appear and disappear at the sides of her mouth — something which had so enchanted Jeremy, and not surprising; heard her laugh at something Bella said; and she thought: this girl is here in place of Jeremy, my tall handsome dearly loved son, and she was married to him for only six months and is already laughing, and perhaps in a year, two years will have almost forgotten him — as I shall never forget him — and will likely marry again and bear more children by some other man, and the episode of her brief marriage to Jeremy will fade into a sad little corner in her early life.

And looking at Cuby in this way, Demelza felt a spasm of resentment within her that in a flash turned almost to hatred.

Judas God! she thought, aghast and sweating, bringing herself up short, what is this I am *thinking*, what is it I am feeling? This girl was the love of Jeremy's heart, and in an ordinary life not cut across by bloody war, would have remained so. She is a *nice* girl, and bearing his child. How can one look beyond that? She has been warm and affectionate to me. Is this feeling I have because, like Clowance, I suspect that if it had not been for her reluctance to marry him, he would not have gone into the army? Or is it something more earthy, more primitive, something every woman feels about another woman who steals her son? In any case it is wrong, wrong, wicked, evil and wrong, and if it is natural to feel it, then I must be unnatural and not *allow* myself to feel it!

I am Ross's wife and Jeremy's mother, not some village woman with mean and narrow and carping thoughts. I am my own person too, separate from Ross, able to choose and decide for myself. Evil thoughts, jealous, mean and petty emotions should be treated like blow-flies, not allowed to settle, driven away. Demelza did not really believe in Sam's circumstantial heaven, with God the Father waiting to greet her; nor really either in Mr Odgers' pallid faith; but if Jeremy's spirit was in any way alive, how humiliated he would be to know that she had harboured such thoughts, even for a moment, about Cuby!

"My dear," she said, "if Clemency would wish to stay for a few days we should be some pleased to have her. Of course you must use the piano whenever you want. It will, I suspicion, be badly out of tune, for I have not used it since — we came home. And even Bella has not been quite in the mood. But it would be lovely to have the

160

sound in the house again."

"That is kind of you," said Clemency. "But Mama will be expecting me home. But if I could come again — and soon . . . "

"Then let us make the most of today," said Bella boisterously.

They made the most of the day, playing and singing for an hour after dinner, and then, under Bella's leadership, took a walk on the beach. Though it was one of the least favourable of days to venture on it, Cuby professed herself delighted with the expanse of sand and sea and rocks, and her cheeks were glowing in an uncommon way for her when she took tea with saffron buns and almond cake in the parlour. Ross talked about the problem of blown sand, especially with north-west winds; down towards Gwithian the sand banks in some places were nearly two hundred feet high and a mile wide. He went on to speak of the plan to extend the pier at St Ives and build a breakwater and the nuisance that town suffered from blown sand. He did not know if his listeners were interested — or indeed if he was very interested himself — but it was something to say and it kept the ball rolling while someone thought up another subject unconnected if possible with the late war.

So the day passed, pleasantly enough as far as it could, nobody upsetting anyone else, but still inevitably much of a social occasion. Nothing could change that except day to day contact on a basis of ordinary living.

In the evening after supper the three girls

had gone to sing duets at the piano, but presently Cuby slipped away, walked through the drawing-room, across the hall and into the parlour, where she found Demelza sitting alone reading a letter.

"Oh, pray excuse me . . . "

"No, no, please to come in. You do not disturb me."

Cuby moved over to a chair, not sure all the same of her welcome.

Demelza said: "It is a letter from Geoffrey Charles. I am only re-reading it. It came on Saturday."

"Oh."

"You met him of course at his party . . . But not since?"

"Not since."

"He is now in the Army of Occupation in Paris. His wife and daughter should be with him by now. He fought all through the Peninsular War and was wounded two or three times, but survived Waterloo without a scratch. Could you do something for me?"

"Of course."

"Those other candles. They will make it more cheerful. Bella and Clemency are playing on alone?"

"Bella is practising that song she sang at the party. 'Ripe Sparrergrass'. She has a fine voice."

"Well, an unusual one. And strong. Her father does not much care for it."

"We all loved it at the party."

"Yes, it is at times like that it shows at its best."

"Do you sing, Lady Poldark?"

"Not now . . . Oh, well, I sang last Christmas — that was the last time. But Bella has quite taken the wind out of my sails!"

"I hope you will sing sometime this Christmas." When Demelza did not reply. "I'm sorry. I should not have said that."

"Perhaps we should all sing because the war is over."

"Yes. I lost my brother at Walcheren."

"I did not know."

Cuby finished lighting the rest of the candles. The old room came into clearer focus, still shabby in spite of new furnishings over the years. It was the room in which all the Poldarks had lived for over three decades. It was the room in which Demelza as a child of fourteen had hidden from her father when he came to take her home to Illuggan.

Demelza was frowning at the letter. "It is strange about Geoffrey Charles that he has made such a fine soldier. He seemed at one time a rather spoilt boy. It was not until he went away to school that he grew up of a sudden, began to change . . . But then . . . "

Cuby sat down and waited. Demelza had been going to say: 'Jeremy was the same.' But it was dangerous ground to walk on. It could not safely be explored yet, if ever.

"He has written to us before — since Waterloo, I mean. In this he just says, 'I nearly and dearly sympathize with you all in your grief.' It is a long, long letter — I think he has specially tried to make it long and interesting — and

163

begins with his account of his march from Waterloo to Paris. He says they marched thirty miles a day! He describes the French peasant women. 'They wore lofty white caps with long flaps hanging down to their shoulders, their exposed stays often not closely laced, bosoms covered with coloured kerchiefs, coarse woollen petticoats striped with pink and reaching only to their calves, with white woollen stockings and sabots. Gold and silver rings in the ears and gold crosses on black ribbons round their necks.' It is a good picture. He says the English troops were welcomed everywhere as a protection against the pillaging of the French soldiers in retreat and the devastation of the brutal Prussians, who tore down doors and windows and burned the furniture in the streets."

"Lady Poldark," Cuby said.

"Yes?"

"May I come and sit next to you?"

"Of course. Of course." Demelza turned over a page. "When they reached Paris they were first encamped in the Bois de Boulogne. Mostly the Prussians, Geoffrey Charles says, were allowed into Paris. He says he is now at a village called St Remy, about twenty-five miles from Paris." She stopped and looked at Cuby, who had come to sit on a stool next to her chair. "But he says he mounted guard in Paris, Geoffrey Charles says, when the Group of Horses which had been stolen from the Venetians were removed from the Arch of Triumph to be returned to their proper owners. Cuby . . . "

"Yes, Lady Poldark?"

"You cannot go on calling me Lady Poldark. I am Jeremy's mother."

"It does not matter. I just want you to know . . ."

"What is it?"

"How much I grieve. Underneath. I put on a pretty show. But underneath."

Demelza said: "Perhaps without him we are both a little hollow."

Cuby put her wet eyes against Demelza's hand.

"I wish I could die."

* * *

Harriet had sent over twice to ask after Stephen's health. Now she wrote:

Dear Clowance,

I understand Stephen is confined to his bed and therefore not suitably to be visited. When he is, pray leave me know, and I will defy the Wrath of God and come to see him. There was a pretty to-do when it was discovered I had been jumping a ditch or so in my present gravid condition; George could not have been more consumed with anger that Stephen had met with an accident riding in my company had Stephen been his dearest friend — which needless to say we all know he is not. A Council of War was held — hardly less than a Star Chamber — with Drs Behenna and Charteris in attendance, in which it was virtually laid down as a Statute

165

*that I should not ride again until after I have
foaled — though Lord save us, it is probably
two months yet to that dreary event.*

*So I send sincerest wishes for your
husband's recovery, and pray let me know
at once if there is anything you lack that I
may provide.*

Cordially yours,
Harriet Warleggan

When Clowance showed it to Stephen he
grunted.

"She may keep her charity. We are well
enough without it."

"I do not think she meant charity in any
ordinary sense — rather, perhaps, books to read
or peaches from their hothouses."

Stephen grunted again. His face was flushed
and his leg painful. "I want nothing more of her
— or any of 'em. I hope she bears him a horse:
that'd suit her, I'll warrant."

Clowance said: "Always before you have been
kindly disposed towards each other. We know
that she helped to deflect George's intention to
bankrupt you. What did she say to you that so
upset you?"

"Forget it."

She waited. "Well, I must reply, thanking her
for her note. When you are better, if you do
not wish to see her then, we can always make
an excuse."

"Can you get me more lemonade? I'm that
thirsty." When she had been for it he said:
"Where's young Jason?"

"He went down with Hodge to see the agents. You remember? He should be back soon."

"Oh, aye, I *remember*. I'm not going to slip my wind yet. Clowance, I been thinking."

"Yes?"

"This Truro Shipping Company that opened up last year. The shares were twenty-five pounds when it began. They're up to thirty-three now. I thought to buy some. Maybe some folk would see them as competitors, but I know the main shareholders and they're friendly along with me. By buying into their business I help my own!"

"So long as you don't overstretch."

He shifted into a more upright position and winced with the pain. "When Swann came up from the Falmouth Naval Bank yesterday he told me what some of the other cargo of the *Revenant* had fetched. Even with the share-out I shall be a richer man than ever I thought. *We* shall be richer. Have you been to the house this week?"

"You know I went yesterday."

Stephen frowned, then half laughed. "Ah, yes. And it is coming along well?"

"Well. Most of the outer structure will be finished by Christmas. We could move in, say, March or April."

"Sooner'n that. Sooner'n that. When am I going to get the use of this leg back? What did Mather say this morning?"

"Yesterday. He said it was only a matter of time . . . "

"Ah, but how much time? That's what I want to know. To come through that privateering venture, wi' folk exploding their muskets in my face, and a French frigate near capturing us, to be floored by a damned horse is the ultimate. Really it is the ultimate . . . "

To calm him Clowance went into details of their house. She had told him them when she came home yesterday, but it lost nothing for him with repetition. Indeed she did not know how much of it he recalled. But when it was over, when she had told him all she could, he was silent for a while. Then he said:

"What'll we call our house, Clowance? Our big beautiful house where we're going to live for the rest of our lives. When we've got those stables up and planted our garden and, maybe, raised our children."

"I don't know," said Clowance. "It's hard to think on a good name."

"Well," Stephen said, "I've a notion. Maybe twill surprise you. But I've a notion to call it Tranquillity."

Clowance looked at him and half smiled.

"Do you think that's what we shall find there?"

Stephen put a hand up to his brow. She came quickly and wiped it for him with a linen towel.

"I don't know," he said. "But that's the name I've the fancy to call it."

★ ★ ★

The sudden improvement in Isabella-Rose's spirits was not without cause. The letter from

168

Geoffrey Charles, which had arrived while Demelza was away, had been accompanied by a second letter addressed to 'Miss Isabella-Rose Poldark', and as her father was out of the house at the time she had been able to spirit it upstairs without anyone seeing it. It was from Christopher Havergal. She did not recognize the writing, and after she had opened it and peeped at the signature she held it to her breast in youthful anxiety before she could bring herself to read.

My dearest, dearest Bella, (it began)
Since I had the inexpressible pleasure of seeing you last, much has happened — most of it disagreeable. I was devastated to hear of the loss of your dear brother. Do you know, I never met him, much as I should have wished to do so. In a large army I suppose it is not surprising that your brother and I did not meet. He was in the 52nd Oxfordshires and I was drafted late into the 73rd Highlanders. On that fateful Sunday his regiment was holding the ground east of Hougoumont whilst we were defending the Ohain road — a distance perhaps of a mile and a half, but a mile and a half more than a little congested with fighting soldiers! (I was nearer Geoffrey Charles, but never saw him either until the Tuesday after.)
I have also lost a part of myself — though not so large a part as rumour, I understand, first had it. We of the 73rd had had a real set-to at Quatre Bras on the Friday (to think I

169

once complained that I had missed most of the war!) but it was not until Sunday afternoon that a cannon-ball arrived and carried off my foot at such a rate that I was never able afterwards to find it, diligently though I searched. My life was saved by a Mrs Bridget O'Hare, wife of Rifleman O'Hare who, like others of her sturdy kind, always follow their husbands into battle. Mercifully no surgeon was about, so I did not lose half my leg; she applied a tourniquet and bound the wound up in dirty rags, and by the time I was picked up by a hospital cart I did not merit surgical attention.

The outcome is that I am minus my left foot, but otherwise intact. I was very soon on crutches, and now, as the breach has healed over, I am beginning to walk with a leather strap and an iron support which I am told will soon be exchanged for an artificial foot. In time maybe even a stick will be superfluous!

I am writing this, as you see, from lodgings in London, where I have had a wonderous convalescent time being fêted and dined in the best houses as one of the young heroes of Glorious Waterloo. In the last five days I have presented myself at my lodgings punctually for breakfast at 9 a.m. — before I went to bed.

Dearest Bella, before you cut me out of your life for such incontinency, I beg to assure you that very, very soon I shall become sober-minded again. But for a little while I *have just rejoiced at being alive and so much in the swim!*

I have to confess to you also, dearest Bella, that I am at present living with a lady! . . .

But she is my landlady — forty years old if she is a day, with bad teeth and a stooping posture — a truly curvilinear old maid, who feeds me well when I am there to be fed and who in all other ways is mercifully unobtrusive. I have seen many charming and pretty and taking young persons since I returned to England, but none has engaged my fancy because in front of them all as I look at them is imposed the utterly enchanting face of my beloved Bella, whose like in the world there is not.

Isabella-Rose Poldark. It reads and speaks most excellently. Isabella-Rose Havergal. That in due course of time, if you will have me, it shall be changed to. But Bella Poldark will always be your stage name. It runs on the tongue. It runs in the mind. As the owner of it will run on the tongue and in the mind of those who eventually see her.

Three months more I shall spend perfecting my New Foot. Riding shall, I swear, be no obstacle. Dancing may prove a trifle more perverse for a while. Aside from that, and a somewhat loping walk, I swear to you I am a whole man — and wholly yours. In three or four months — perhaps in the spring when your flowers are out — I shall come and sample the salutiferous air of Cornwall.

Then, my lovely poppet, I shall hope to see you again!

Your devoted friend — who wishes in due time to be more,

Christopher Havergal

11

I T was Music Thomas's wedding day.
Or rather it was the day on which it had
been proposed he should be joined in holy
matrimony to his dearly loved and admired
Katie Carter, when they would cleave together
and be of one flesh — or at least live together
and be of one cottage — until death did them
part. Now, alas, not a death but the failure of
an expected birth had prevented the union being
proceeded with. Katie had let him down, as no
doubt she'd the right to do, or so Surgeon Enys
said, and he did ought to know. But the rights
or wrongs of the situation helped Music not at
all. The desire of his life — although it had
seemed far out of his reach — had suddenly
been promised him. Now it was as suddenly
withdrawn. And he had become the laughing
stock of the village.

At twelve noon on his wedding day Music
stood in his cottage staring round it, all so clean
and so tidy and lovingly repaired. Night after
night, and whenever he could get away, he had
worked to make the place suitable for his queen.
Now it was empty except for his four cats.

It was worse being so clean, so tidy; and his
brothers would be sneering. The sun was falling
through the new windows he had put in. Good
glass had been hard to come by, so he had
puttied in a piece of bottle-green glass for the

lower panes; with the sun shining through it it looked the colour of sea water with bubbles. (Upstairs in the bedroom he had had to make do with oiled paper.)

And the privy was clean and the steps to it new laid, and the back plot was as tidy as could be expected with three hens roaming it, and beyond that Will Nanfan's field and then the moors leading to the cliffs with the Queen Rock looming out at sea.

He knew he should be at Place House, for it was not his official time off, but he did not stir. If he was sacked he didn't any longer care. He'd get a job, some sort of a job, to keep himself fed — if there was any purpose now in staying fed. Many folk, of course, had been against the idea of his wedding Katie; her mother had and her brother had and her grandfolk had; they'd all thought he wasn't good enough. There was a time when he had greatly admired Ben Carter — still did in some ways: that there organ he'd built all by his self in his own bedroom. They was clever folk, the Carters, not like him, the village fool, singing alto and walking spring-heeled and anyone could make a butt of him.

Yet she'd promised. She'd scat her promise. She said she'd wed him and now would not. The Carters were no betterer than the Thomases. In fact worse, for he'd never gone back on no promise to no one.

He'd helped Ben Carter when he'd been in trouble that time, when he'd met him coming out of The Bounders' Arms, with Emma Hartnell propping him up and him

174

as drunk as a newt; he'd helped him back to his mother's shop and helped him upstairs, and Katie had come upon them and had given Music a rare old talking to for helping himself to the asparagus in the walled garden of Place House to take as a present to Dr Enys. But it had all ended beautiful. It had all ended with Katie giving him a kiss — the only one ever, and he had galloped back to Place House like a man who'd found a gold mine.

That was the best day of all. It had never been so good after, with Katie only having eyes for Saul Grieves and Grieves only having eyes for any slip or mistake or shortcoming Music might have or make. It had been sneer, sneer all the way.

Music had never seen Ben Carter tipsy drunk before, nor never since, and his brother John had said it was because Clowance Poldark had gone off to wed that up-country sailor feller, Stephen Carrington. Crossed in love Ben had been, not just so different from Music's own plight now. But ne'er as *bad*. Ne'er as *bad*. Music would have taken his oath Miss Clowance Poldark could *never* have promised to wed Ben, let alone scat it up at the last minute. Ben had got tipsy drunk all the same. Why not? Why shouldn't *he* get tipsy drunk today? He'd pennies enough. He'd been saving for the marriage day, and Surgeon Enys had been generous about those shelves. And that wonderful lady whose dog him and Miss Clowance had helped to bring home in the snow last February, that wonderful lady, Lady Something, had given him more money than he had ever had before in his life.

Rum. That was what Emma Hartnell had said Ben had been drinking all day. Music had only touched spirits three times in his life but he'd never tasted rum. Maybe twas the best thing to fill up a hollow heart.

But where to get it? There was Sally Chill-Off's, just at the head of the Combe. Emma's the other way, past the church. A half-dozen more to choose from. But which might turn him away afore he had had his fill? They cared naught, none of 'em cared naught so long as he had the pennies and they didn't have to chalk up his debt on the side of the bellows. Ned Hartnell was the most likely to see him away too soon. The Bounders' Arms was a bit superior against the rest. But that was where Ben had gone. That was where Music thought he was least likely to meet the village lads. If Ned and Emma would let him he would drink himself quickly into a state where everything would be forgot.

★ ★ ★

Three hours later Ned edged him out of the side door of the inn. Music was a mite frustrated, because he had wanted to be just so far gone as Ben had been, and then Emma could've helped him all the way home. It would have been nice to have leaned on Emma all the way home, because she was soft and kindly and he might have got his arm around her waist even if only in the most chaste way. In fact, though he did not know it, Ned had substantially watered his

176

rum, not wishing to have the young man snoring under his table for the next twelve hours.

Still, he was distinctly merry and the emptiness and grief had disappeared. And he was unsteady enough for Ned to lend him a stick. *And* they'd been all strangers in the inn — that is from places more than a mile away, like Marasanvose and Bargus — so they'd not tormented him with jokes about the wedding.

In the left pocket of his rough smock he carried a small flask. When he got home he reckoned if he finished that off he would sleep his way into oblivion for the rest of the day.

Fine morning, wet evening, that's what it was going to be. The sun had sneered its way behind some mackerel clouds, and there were heavier ones creeping up.

Creeping up, that was the word. Something hit him on the shoulder. It was a clod of earth. He turned slowly, trying to keep his balance, and there was a titter. It was a girlish titter and after a moment or two another piece, half stone, half grass, hit him on the leg. He recognized the black tousled head of Lily Triggs. Then he saw Mary Billing and Susie Bice. Others began to appear out of the rough gorse and outcroppings of rock.

"Goin' church, Music, are ee? Can we come 'long and see the fun? Like to wed one of us, would ee, now? How 'bout Mary 'ere? She'm a fine maid, she be. Just ripe for ee! Heh! Heh! Heh!"

He waved his stick, half in menace, half in fun and then went on. But in front of him he found five big lads barring his way. Another Bice, another Billing, and Joe Stevens, who was one of his long-term tormentors.

"Let's all go church, shall us," said Stevens. "Be ee bride or groom, Music?" He tried to hang a lump of turf with trailing ends on Music's head. "Crown 'im, crown 'im!"

Music knocked the turf away and lost his hat. He pushed his way through the lads and went on his way. He was near the church, and was almost up to the churchyard when his arms were seized.

It was the girls who had got hold of him — hard and noisy as the lads — but because they were women he could not very well knock them away. He struggled to be free, but his fumed head let him down and he fell. Hands grabbed him again and he was yanked to his feet. Laughing, jeering faces.

"Come us on, me dears. Getten wed are ee? Set 'im down in church porch, and ye can wait for yer bride!"

Struggling they lugged him into the church-yard and half-way to the church. Stevens tore up another hummock of grass and clumped it on his head; it stayed there while they howled with laughter. There were now a dozen or more, dancing round him jeering at him and thumping him. He aimed a couple of swinging blows: one landed on Stevens, the other floored Mary Billing, who got in the way at the last moment.

They didn't dare frog march him into the church, but Mary Billing, scrambling to her feet, screamed: "Put'n in the stocks! That'll learn un. Let'n spend 'is wedden day setten in the churchyard!"

Not far from the porch of the church was a pair of stocks and beside it a whipping post. The post was not often used but the stocks were accepted as a valuable corrective for the minor miscreant.

Struggling and wriggling and dizzy with drink, Music was hauled towards the stocks; he would have been a handful to force into them, but at the wrong moment Mary Billing charged him head down like a bull and knocked all the wind out of him. By the time he began to get it back his ankles were secured, and then it was only a bit more struggling before his arms were fixed into the appropriate holes.

The lads and the girls — six of one and nine of the other — now stood back and looked at their victim. They screamed with laughter, disturbing the rooks overhead. It was the best joke they'd had for years, and into it came a half-realized resentment against the village fool who had striven to shake off his image. While he had been ready to play the idiot, singing alto at the head of any procession they got up, capering like a loon on the balls of his feet, ready to be laughed at because it was the only claim he would ever have to notoriety, he was a popular figure. But these last two years the fun had gone out of him; except for church he wouldn't sing at all; he had begun walking more or less ordinary; he'd put on a few airs, trying to distance himself from his old reputation; and all this had come to a head by him having the cheek to think he could wed a capable girl like Ben Carter's sister. Now she'd jilted him and good luck to her; that'd learn him. And this'd learn him too.

Of all people it was Susie Bice who threw the first handful of gravel at him. The Bices were not a nice family — shiftless and ailing and far from honest — but Susie had always been thought to be the best of a poor lot. It is doubtful now if she thought to start anything serious, but that was how it began. One after another the group began to pick up anything they could find in the churchyard and pelt Music with it.

Then Joe Stevens said: "Nay, let's play fair. Let's draw a line, see. No one afore that line. No cheaten. We tak it from this yur line, see who scores a hit. See — "

"Stick a pipe in 'is mouth!" screamed Mary Billing excitedly. "Make 'im into an Aunt Sally!"

"Nay, he'd never 'old un. Leave'n be."

"Nay, let's dress im all golden like wi' gorse prickles, ready for 'is wedden."

But Stevens and Bert Bice had no time for frills. They had drawn their line and were beginning to aim. And the one thing available was just beneath a headstone to old Dr Choake. The grave was covered with grey pebbles.

★ ★ ★

The Warleggans — Valentine and Selina, that is — had engaged a housekeeper called Mrs

Alice Treffrey to take charge of Place House while they were in Cambridge. Mrs Treffrey came as senior parlourmaid from Tehidy, with the highest references, and there was not likely to be a repeat of Saul Grieves's misbehaviour. Because she was new to the job she did not notice the absence of the stableman; but others did. Katie — whose waistline had by now almost resumed its normal dimensions — could not get away until well on into the afternoon; then she went in search of him. She thought it might be his 'purty chets' that were keeping him. Or, the day being what it was, he might just be sulking. Anyway there was no call for him to lose his job: she would soon root him out, knock some sense into him.

The cottage was empty. Even the cats were not to be seen, though when she went out of the back door she thought she spotted a vanishing tail. She went through and out to the front. In the next cottage were the formidable Paynters, and Prudie was leaning over the wall.

"Looking for lover?" she asked with a leer.

Katie caught a glimpse through the open door of the lamentable Jud filling his pipe.

"I be seeking Music, if that's what ye d'mean."

"He be gone that way," said Prudie with a sweep of a fat wobbly arm.

The sweep covered an area of about a quarter of the compass, but there were virtually only two tracks leading in that general direction: one towards the ruined engine house of Grambler and thence to Nampara, the other to the church.

Katie chose the church, and very soon heard excited cries and whoops from inside the lych gate. A few strides inside and she came on a group of lads and girls, in their late teens and early twenties, excitedly, hysterically egging each other on to stone her *ci-devant* fiancé imprisoned in the stocks. There had been a number of good hits and blood was running down his face. He was struggling to get out.

Not far from this scene was an open grave, ready dug but not yet occupied. Beside the mound of clay and stones (some of the stone bearing unmistakable gleams of mineral) was the shovel Jan Triggs, the present sexton, had been using. It was a type known as a 'lazy back', having a long handle and a heart-shaped blade. Katie picked it up, twisted it round in her hands to get a firm grip, walked back and knocked Joe Stevens unconscious with a tremendous swing to the head. Then she swung back the other way and caught Bert Bice in the chest, breaking two of his ribs. Mary Billing just dodged a blow that would almost have decapitated her, and the rest simply dropped the stones and fled.

Katie flung the shovel aside and went up to the stocks. Music blinked up through the blood at his new tormentor.

"Get out o' thur, ye great drunken fool!" she shouted in a fine temper. "Cor, I can catch your breath a mile away — "

"Katie, I done me bestest — "

"Bestest, is it, an? My dear soul, I'd dearly not wish to know your worst! Come us on, come us on! . . . "

She lifted the wooden frame and helped him out of the stocks. A stray stone hit the woodwork as she did so, but she looked up with a glare so fierce no more followed. Two youths were kneeling beside Joe Stevens, who was stretched out on the grass just beginning to groan. Bert Bice was being helped away, holding his chest.

Free of the stocks, Music fell back on the grass and then made an effort to struggle to his feet.

"Lay still, ye gurt fool! Blinded your eyes, 'ave they? I'll see the magistrates 'bout that; have 'em up — "

"Nay, Katie, I can see well 'nough. Tis only the blood from these yur cuts on me 'ead. See." He smeared his face with the back of his hand and blinked up apologetically at her. He might still smell strongly of rum, but his ordeal had gone a way to sobering him up.

Katie took off her yellow kerchief and began to wipe his face. It emerged through the blood and the dirt.

"Stinking great labbats," she said, stopping to glare behind her. Two lads were half helping, half carrying Joe Stevens out of the danger zone. Presently they were all gone. She stood hands on hips staring belligerently around her, then turned her attention to the wounded man.

"Get on up, can ee?" She helped him to his feet. He lurched against her, then straightened himself. "Come us on; I'll put ee home."

It was not a long way — nothing to the distance Music had aided Ben to walk on a previous occasion. They reached the cottage.

Luckily Prudie had gone in, and all the people in the cottage on the other side were at work. It was beginning to rain.

"Ye gurt *fool*," said Katie again. "What d'ye want to go get drunk for? Sit *down*!" she commanded. "I'll get ee a dish of water to bathe off your face. And I'll boil a pan — make ee some tay. Not as I'd not be above one myself!" Her own hands were trembling with the spent anger.

She brought him a bowl and then while he dabbed at himself she lit the fire with some shavings and pieces of driftwood.

She sat back on her heels, looking at the fire. "My, don't it draw!"

When she had come back from the pump for a second time with water to make the tea, she glanced at Music who had finished dabbing and was drying his face on a duster.

"That won't do! That's a halfy job. Ere take yer shirt off. And yer breeches. You're all caked and cabby."

He reluctantly removed his shirt and she looked at the muscles rippling in his arms.

"My, what a gurt man ye are! Look, I reckon Surgeon Enys should tend this wound in yer 'ead. Tis gaping like a little mouth."

"Tis narthing, Katie. Reelly. I'll go Irby's and he'll put some salve on it."

"We'll see 'bout that. Now yer breeches."

Music looked at her sidelong. "Cain't do tha-at. I got no slights on."

"Well, land sakes, fraid o' me seeing something, are ee? Giss along. Ere — this

184

cloth'll do. Draw off yer breeches and wrap'n round like a skirt. Ere, I'll tak yer boots off. If ye bend too far twill open up the bleeding."

So presently he was sitting with a piece of old tablecloth round his middle and a potato sack over his shoulders while she made the tea. There were two clean cups he'd bought for the wedding and a half jug of milk the cats had not been able to get at.

They sat there in silence for a few minutes, drinking the hot tea. It was raining heavily now and a rising wind beat the rain against the coloured window panes.

"Them Bices, them Billings," said Katie, "they should be learned a lesson."

"Reckon they 'ave been," said Music with a half-giggle. "An' Joe Stevens. He's always one in the lead."

"Ah. Well, I've give 'im a sore 'ead."

"I'll mind it fur a long time," said Music, sipping at his tea. "I'll mind it fur a long time. You thur striking of 'em, this way, that way, they went down like ninepins." He relished the phrase. "Just like ninepins."

Katie poured out more tea, stirred each cup with the one wooden spoon. "I'd best be getting back. Else they'll think I've fell down a shaft. I'll tell 'em ye met wi' an accident. Mind you come first thing tomorrow."

"Ais. Oh ais, I will that. I will that, Katie."

"Not that Mrs Treffrey will scold. She'm easy-going for time so long as the work d'get done."

"I'll be there, Katie, sure 'nough."

Katie looked at him. "You're a fine figure, ain't you? Gotten more clothes upstairs, 'ave ee?"

"No. Well . . . I've a jacket and breeches 'anging on the wall, but that's for Sunday."

Katie went up and fetched them. She held them up for inspection and dropped them on the table. "Let's look at yer 'ead."

She examined him again. "You should see Surgeon for that. It d'keep welling up. Aside from that . . . "

"Ais, Katie." He smiled at her.

She stared at him again. "Reckon if I'd wed you you'd 've drove me mad."

"Stay a space longer," urged Music. "Look at'n. Tis enting down."

"Put yer clothes on, then," said Katie. "You'll catch yer death."

He dragged off into the scullery and presently emerged in his Sunday best. His face was a mess, three bruises and two cuts, but his eyes clear again, at their most dazed blue.

"Reckon ye need someone to look for you," said Katie contemptuously. "You're as fazy as yer cats."

"No," said Music.

The firmness of his voice surprised her. It was the first time he had contradicted her.

"*I* want to look for *you*," said Music. "All the time — from daystrike to nightgleam. Tha's what I allus wanted for to do. All the time. Tis still what I want for to do."

An extra flurry of rain lashed on the glass.

"You reckon that, do you?" said Katie.

"Yes, I do."

Katie thought for a long time.

"You'd drive me mad," she eventually said.

A smile cracked his battered face. "Nay, Katie, I wouldn't. Honest I wouldn't."

12

ON Friday, the 13th October Stephen was brighter than he had been for several days, and he seemed no longer in pain. He talked a lot to Clowance, though it was not always coherent.

"I've come a long way with you already," he said, "and there's big plans for next year and the year after. I been thinking them over all this time I've been laid up. For you and Jason and the Carrington line. I shall build another vessel, that's what I shall do, one to me own specifications, give the *Lady Clowance* over to Jason. Now the war's really over it looks as if we shall have peace in our lifetime, so we must bend our ways to make the *best* of peace. Peaceful trade's profitable if you get in when the tide's making, before your rivals. Great thing is not to work for other folk but to work for yourself. Then ye don't get paid per week — per month — ye get what ye've earned and it goes into no one else's pocket. I'm thinking to start a Joint Stock Company."

"What is that?"

"Tis a more modern way of adventuring as in a mine. Or taking shares in a privateer. You establish a Joint Stock Company of say five thousand pounds and you keep three thousand of the stock in your own hands. Others invest in the shares and take a share of the profit, but

188

you always keep control. That way you have the use of two thousand pounds of their money at no cost to yourself. It was the same sort of idea I thought on when I was in hock to Warleggan's. Then no one wanted a share. It will be different now."

He licked his lips, and she wiped his face and gave him a sip of lemonade.

He chuckled. "I've been clever in me life, y'know. Clever this last year or so. I reckon you've brought me luck, dear heart. All along, you've brought me luck."

When did your first wife die? she wanted to ask, and was she dead in 1813, when you were first going to marry me, or were you just resolved to take a chance on not being found out? She wanted harshly, desperately to ask, but instead she wiped his brow again and moistened his dry lips.

He said: "I've been in one or two scrapes, as ye well know. And some ye know not of. That first time when we were at the races and Andrew recognized me as the man in the bar at Plymouth Dock . . . . It was a nasty moment. I've never been too sure of Andrew, y'know. He means well, most of the time, but he talks too much and is leaky in his liquor. Let him drop the wrong word when George Warleggan or one of his creatures is around . . . But now I no longer fear his indiscretions. He's sobering up with Tamsin, and it is all disappearing into the distant past. Like — like something else that happened that he was not concerned in. Others were. Ye'd be surprised if I told you who the others were. Someone quite close to you. But I never will, never can now . . . "

Jason put his head round the door. "I'll spell you while you take your dinner, ma'am."

Clowance went to the door. "I cannot come yet. And — I think you should go for Dr Mather."

"Why? Is he . . . ?"

"Tell him I would like him to come."

When she returned to the bed Stephen was smiling again.

"Ye're real good to me, dear heart. I don't know what I did to deserve a wife like you. What was I saying?"

"It does not matter, Stephen. Try to rest."

"Oh, I know. About me old luck. Look you, there was Plymouth Dock, and I was well out of that. Then there was the stage — the other thing, and I was well out of that. Then George Warleggan and his toadies tried to bankrupt me and drew back at the very last, and I was well out of that. Then there was the privateering adventure, which has made our fortune. And a Frenchie discharged his musket full in me face, and the charge was wet . . . Now I have fallen off a damned, cursed horse and hurt me back, but that is over now and I will soon be well out of that. We're turning up the aces, dear heart, aren't we now?"

"Yes," said Clowance, sitting quietly down again.

"A leaky ship and the anchor's down. Hurrah me lads, hurrah." Stephen was trying to sing.

"Hush, my dear, do not tire yourself."

190

He was quiet for a minute or so, then he said: "I reckon twelve pounds for a spring be too much. Why I can take it Plymouth and get it done for less. I reckon tis always the way; your local port'll try to charge too much. In dry dock, ye say? I'm poxed if she needs dry dock." Then a little later: "Swedish pitch at eleven shillings a hundredweight and Russian tar at twenty shillings a barrel. Can ye match that?"

Friday the 13th. Clowance was not superstitious but the day had the lowering look of the end of summer, the end of hope. From this window she could see a corner of the cottage roof next door, a piece of sky with clouds as dark as coal smoke shredding across it, and a lip of the harbour curling with spiteful little waves. She was filled with dread for the future; all the warm hopes of last year were gone and she lived in a spider's web of sadness and suspicion. Everywhere where there had been certainty there were shifting sands. She had never felt so much alone in an alien world.

"What I want," said Stephen, addressing someone outside the room, "is a smart little cabin for the master, bulkheads half panelled in maple and teak. And then in the corner a fine settee upholstered in crimson plush, see? A neat fireplace and maybe a tiled surround wi' a brass mantelshelf." Now he turned his head suddenly: "That suit ye, Clowance? Care to come wi' me across to Brittany? What shall we name her, eh? Now we've got a *Lady Clowance*, maybe we could call her the *Lady Carrington*?

The flagship of the Carrington line!"

"I'd love to come," said Clowance, "when she's built. Get well first."

"Oh, I'm coming along fine. Where's Jason?"

"Just gone out to fetch me something."

"Reckon she'll carry a crew of eight, the *Lady Carrington*. That is about the style . . . Frame shall be of English oak planks; deck, I reckon, of Quebec yellow pine. Very even and hard wearing. The oak can be got from the Tamar River and shipped from Plymouth. Masts of Canadian red pine; yards, topmasts, jib-boom the same. Diameter? I can't tell ye that till we've got the full plan! Where's Jason?"

"He'll be back soon."

Stephen looked at her with a strange expression in his eyes. "Tell him to hurry."

"I will, I will."

"She shall be laid down in Falmouth," he said. "Bennett's is a better yard than Carne's in Looe, bigger. Sorry, for your father has a money share in Carne's."

"No matter."

"Will ye hold my hand," he said.

She drew her chair nearer to the bed and took his hand, which was moist and had no strength in the grip.

"That Frenchie," he said, with a chuckle that rustled in his throat. "Ye should've seen his face when the musket did not fire. I stabbed him through the chest. Blade went in so far I could not withdraw the knife. Biggest killing I've ever done, yet folk *praise* me for that. Don't make sense. Clowance, ye're a rare good wife.

Where's . . . young . . . Jason?"

His head sank back on the pillows and his breathing became heavy and irregular. When Jason came back with Dr Mather, Stephen was unconscious. It was a long fight then; a man, still young, whose powerful body struggled against the forces of disintegration that attacked it. The hours passed and the night passed in this tremendous contest while the passionate need to live was slowly eroded by a relentless escape of blood. Dawn broke before it was over.

Book Four

1

L ETTER from Jeremy Poldark to his mother, handed to her by Cuby Poldark the day Cuby returned to Caerhays.

Brussels, 1st June 1815

Dearest Mother,

I do not suppose you will ever receive this letter — certainly I trust you shall not! — but just in case I thought to leave it in safer hands than mine.

In January 1812 I indulged in an adventurous caper that I feel by some alchemy of your own you have already partly apprehended. I will not go into details, for whatever I said your apprehension would never become comprehension. For I do not altogether understand it myself. A serious law was broke by three persons, of whom I was one. I will say no more except to make it clear — and this is one of the purposes of this letter — that I was not unduly influenced by the other two. If anything I was rather the motivating force, and I worked out the plan that was carried out. If you suspect who the others might be, do not consider them more to blame than I and indeed rather the less.

Nor should adverse circumstances be held to carry any more than a small load of responsibility. Of course I was disturbed and restless and unhappy. But that was only a scattering of gunpowder on the floor: there was no need to scrape it together and light a fuse! I wish I were able to explain it better than that — I cannot. Did I have an ancestor who ended up as a highwayman dangling at the end of a rope?

One thing is certain. You are in no way at all to blame, nor is my father. I had a splendid childhood and a carefree youth-time. Any worm in the bud existed before the fruit was set.

That is all — let us not be pompous about it. If, as I trust, I return with Cuby to set up house together near you, you will never see this — though perhaps it assuages something in me merely to write it down, believing that it will never be read by the Person to whom it is addressed. But then, on my return to Nampara, and at an early stage, I shall reclaim from you a little Loving Cup that you say you found one day on the beach; and I shall look on it as a cup of good fortune and keep it somewhere safe in my own home. If you should read this letter, then perhaps it has rather been a cup of Ill-Fortune, and, since you say you picked it from the sea, to the sea it should be returned.

By the way, last Christmas Valentine was asking me about installing an engine for his new mine, Wheal Elizabeth. If I am not about, tell him to approach Arthur Wolff, who is really the first man nowadays. Tell Valentine on no account to put in a plunger poll engine;

they work excellent to begin but the exposure of the whole piston to the atmosphere at every stroke is unsound practice and will lead to excessive wear.

Well, this is about all I have to say! It is my usual custom to end my letters on a jolly note, but clearly this cannot be so in a letter which, if jollity prevail, you will never see! So may I just end with a charge to you and Father to care for Cuby and for our child? I know you will do this without any request from me, so pray take any more as said. Cuby is a wonderful girl and a wonderful wife — there could be no better — who is only just coming into her own. I would not want her to regress under any Influence her elder brother might exert. You, Mama, I think, would be the greatest influence — after me! — in inducing her not to do so.

Love, love, love to you all.

Jeremy

★ ★ ★

Letter to Sir Ross Poldark from George Canning.

Caldas, Portugal,
25th September 1815

My dear Friend,

Thank you for your letter in reply to mine of the 8th July. In expressing our sympathy to you and your wife and family over your grievous loss we were only joining in the chorus of loving friends who must have written in the same vein to try to support and comfort you all. Though I have met none of your family — except briefly your beautiful daughter at the Duchess of Gordon's Ball — I feel that you have always been a close and loving entity, and the loss of your eldest son will be a sword thrust that will wound you to the heart.

But my dear friend, this second letter of yours grieves me in another way because it speaks of your intended withdrawal from public life and your decision to live henceforward in your Cornish home seeing to your own affairs. In large — at least in part — I can only commend such a decision — for what else have I done? — and I know of your long formulated intention to leave Parliament at the successful conclusion of the French wars. That is as it should be. You are not the political animal I am.

But you have so much to bring to public life in some form — a strength of character, a rare integrity, a thinking brain which does not allow itself to be diverted from its true concerns, a passionate belief in freedom and justice, a resolution in all good things: these are in such rare supply today that they cannot, shall not, I hope, be altogether lost to those of us who inhabit the world of affairs.

Peace, I have no more to say, except to ask you in due time, in God's good time, to think carefully on what I write. As for myself, what you may imagine am I doing with my own life to preach to a better man? The answer is little enough. At the end of June I wrote to the Government offering my resignation as Ambassador here, and a month later they accepted it. Now that the menace of Napoleon has finally been removed there is no need to keep such a large embassy in being in Lisbon, so they are going to scale it down and leave it to a chargé d'affaires. And I have become a private citizen!

One of my main reasons for accepting the post in Portugal in the first place was on account of George's delicate health, and in the hope that the warmth should suit him. It does. So I have brought him to Caldas to the warm baths. You will understand — and forgive me for — such a preoccupation with our eldest son. Here it is even hotter than Lisbon, and Joan and the little ones have fled to Cintra where the sea breezes blow. But George prospers in the heat, so I shall stay as long as he is happy here.

For the future? Of course I must return to England, temporarily or permanently, in the new year, if only to assuage my Liverpool constituents, who have seen nothing of me all this time! I do not yet feel ready to resume my political career (nor is there any inducement to do so), so probably I shall return to Portugal and then we shall travel into other parts of Europe — Madrid, Rome, Naples, Florence. Do you know you are luckier in one respect than I am, for I have never been to Paris.

But one day early next year I may of a

201

sudden arrive in Falmouth — on my own, the family will stay here — and I do not know how far your home is from that port but in so narrow a county it can hardly be farther than a day's ride. By then, my dear friend, I trust you and your wife will have come through the worst of your tragic bereavement. At least let us talk, and if you are adamant in your decision I shall henceforward hold my peace.

Believe me, with all sympathy and much admiration,

your Sincere Friend,
George Canning

PS I am sure you will take great satisfaction from the news that Fouché has now fallen — disgraced, I hear — and Tallien with him. So the stables are being cleaned at last!

★ ★ ★

Stephen Carrington was buried at St Gluvias Parish Church on the 19th October, the Reverend John Francis Howell officiating. A great many people turned out. In his short time in Penryn Stephen had become widely known, and on the whole well liked. Falmouth and Penryn, being ports, were more used to the abrupt arrival and departure of strangers and therefore were less clannish, at least on a superficial level. Stephen had had a 'way' with him, had been free with his money, talked with high and low alike, had put business in the way of the towns, and most recently had achieved

202

a remarkable privateering success which had enriched both those who had put money into his adventure and the men who sailed with him.

There were also mourners from Truro, and Andrew and Verity Blamey, and a large north-coast contingent which included Ross and Demelza and Isabella-Rose, Dwight and Caroline Enys, Will and Char Nanfan. There were a few of his gambling and hunting friends — Anthony Trefusis and Percy Hill and George and Thomasine Trevethan. His nephew, Jason Carrington, stood beside Clowance all the time, tears running unchecked down his cheeks. On the edge of things, sidling into a corner of the church and keeping her distance at the graveside, was Lottie Kempthorne. Neither George nor Harriet was there, but a slim nervous lawyer called Hector Trembath had come to represent them.

Clowance went through it all with a white, drawn face but tearless eyes. When it was over the Trevethans, whose large house was near the church, invited relatives and friends to a light meal, then everyone dispersed. Clowance had been staying with Verity: she said she would ride back with her father and mother that night and stay two or three days at Nampara, then she would return to Penryn where there was much to see to. Demelza said: "Let your father do it; he will willingly do it; there is no reason for you to return at all, except to pack a few belongings."

"I want to see to things myself, Mama. There is so much to think about; I haven't decided what to do about anything yet. *Anything.*"

She stayed three nights and then rode home. She had an open invitation from Verity but she decided for the time being to live at the cottage at Penryn. Demelza persuaded her to take Betsy Maria Martin with her, a solution Clowance said she willingly accepted of. She liked Betsy Maria, and another woman for company was welcome. She told her mother that she would stay at Penryn at least until after Christmas.

Demelza said to Ross: "I think she may be stopping away because of Cuby." Cuby was returning to Nampara in November.

"It is not so simple as that," Ross said. "I know there is this little bitterness on Clowance's part. But Clowance has suffered two of the hardest blows a woman can receive — the loss of a brother and the loss of a husband — within a bare four months. She's a very brave, honest person, and I think she just wishes to face it alone."

"Cuby too has lost a brother and a husband," said Demelza. "She is more hurt than she shows, Ross."

"The child may help *her* — it must help her."

Demelza sighed. "We are a sorry lot. Thank God for *our* children — what is left of 'em . . . Bella continues to bubble — she has quite recovered her spirits. And little Henry is a joy. One day, maybe, we shall learn to be happy with the blessings that are left."

★ ★ ★

In November the weather turned foul; there were storms up and down the coast, accompanied by the usual shipwrecks. A barque was wrecked off the Lizard with a loss of eight lives; she carried woollens and worsteds and refined sugar. Another vessel foundered near Padstow, with Indian spices, ivory, tea and sandalwood. A third with timber ran on the rocks at Basset's Cove. Hendrawna, wide open though it was to accept suitable offerings, only received some of the flotsam from ships lost elsewhere.

Katie and Music were to be married on Saturday the 11th November, which was Martinmas. When the news leaked out that Katie had relented and was taking Music from choice and not from necessity, the neighbourhood heard it first with derision and then with resignation. Sentiment is as changeable as the wind, and apart from a few of the girls and youths who had taunted Music, the general feeling swung in his support. The lad must have *something* about him for Katie to show him this favour. Maybe he'd proved a thing or two to Katie that we don't know nothing about. Maybe she'd best make sure of her man this time before something *really* turns up!

The only actual resentment came from Bradley Stevens, Joe Stevens's father, and some of the girls. Joe Stevens still had dizzy spells and Bert Bice's ribs were mending slowly. The week before the wedding, when the banns had been called for the third time, they got together in a group after church and thought out how best they might disrupt the wedding.

They could create a disturbance in church, but Parson Odgers was so much in his dotage he would hardly notice, and anyway Music would only grin feebly and Katie glower; the ceremony would be carried on even in a pandemonium. Also it was rumoured that Dr Enys was going to be present, and although he was not a magistrate he knew all the magistrates. You didn't if possible tangle with the gentry. After the ceremony as they came out of church you could pelt them with mud, of which there was plenty after last week's storms, but again Dr Enys might be there and receive an ill-directed volley. Before the ceremony offered the better chances. Katie had to walk up from Sawle with her mother and her step-father (supposing they agreed to accompany her — Ben would certainly not be there); Music had a much shorter distance to come and might come alone (it was rumoured he'd had hard words with his brothers). They could get some liquid manure ready in pails and swamp him as he came up the hill. Then when he'd gone into church all sodden and stinking they'd barrow in a dozen loads of pig shit and dump it all over his cottage. This plan, the brain-child of Mary Billing, was acclaimed by all.

The day before, Ross had ridden over to the Blowing House near Truro, in which he had a substantial share. He had dinner with two of the other partners and then met Dwight Enys at the Red Lion and they rode home together.

Dwight said: "From the beginning there was nothing any surgeon could do for Stephen except wait. If a man is injured in the head, one may attempt a trepan, if one of the limbs, at worst one can amputate; for the spine there is virtually nothing. In his case — though neither Mather nor I thought it suitable to ask that we might open the body — we were both certain it was internal bleeding which led to his death."

"Clowance was devoted to him," Ross said, "and they were happy together. He was a brave man and was becoming a successful one. After all his adventures and risky enterprises it is a cynical tragedy he should die in this useless and silly way."

"I understand from Caroline that Harriet was much upset by the accident and has been more or less confined to the house since, not by infirmity but by George's edict. He is putting much store on the birth of this new baby."

"They tell me he made a fortune out of Waterloo," Ross said drily.

"'Dost thou laugh to see how fools are vex'd to add to golden numbers golden numbers?'"

"What is that?"

"Something I was reading last night."

"Isn't there a verse in the Bible about the ungodly flourishing like a green bay tree?"

Dwight smiled. "We all must learn to flourish as best we can, I suppose. And it's good to be able to survive, even in a more modest fashion, as we both do, with somewhat clearer consciences than George must have."

"I do not suppose that George's conscience ever caused him the loss of a moment's sleep. What would cause him loss of sleep would be if he felt he had paid half a guinea too much for a horse he was buying from a starving farmer."

The track separated them. The mid-afternoon was frowning towards evening, and it would be dark before they reached home.

When they came together again Dwight said: "You will have heard that Music Thomas is to marry Katie Carter tomorrow."

"Yes."

"I hope it may turn out well. I think it might. For Katie to marry Music willingly makes an altogether better prospect of it."

"Ben does not feel so."

"It was about that that I wanted to speak to you, Ross. I know you've long had an interest in the Carter family, as indeed I have. We both remember our visit to Launceston gaol."

"I often think", said Ross, "it is due to your ministrations that Zacky is still alive."

"Zacky is alive because he has a constitution which will not give way; my medicaments are no more than a useful prop. But I think Katie will be grieved if no one of her family — except her mother, and she reluctantly — comes to the church ... I suppose Ben is unrelenting ... and I doubt if Zacky could walk that distance. But Mrs Zacky is a devout Wesleyan and goes regularly to church. Do you have any leverage you could exercise?"

"Only persuasion. Which I will exercise since it is you that asks. Betsy Maria is in Penryn with Clowance, but there are a half-dozen uncles and aunts — some of them younger than Katie — who might be willing to go. And of course there are the Nanfans. I'll see what I can do."

"Thank you."

"I don't recall having seen Music for a couple of years, and then he was still very much the village fool."

"I've no doubt that if you were to call to see him now, he would be so overcome with embarrassment that you'd think him no better. And I rather fear that the excitement of the wedding may tip his balance tomorrow. But not only has he improved, he is still improving. Rather than being mentally retarded, as we all thought, I am convinced he is just a very slow developer, whose development has been much held back by the part he learned to play and what the village expected of him. I think with Katie's understanding and companionship he may become at least as normal and intelligent as most of those who taunt him."

By the time they separated the night's cloak had been drawn over the sky with just a scarf of daylight reaching into the sea. Ross made a short detour to Mellin and knocked at the Martin cottage. So he had come one morning thirty years ago in search of cheap labour to work his neglected fields, and so had met Jinny for the first time and become involved in the fortunes of the whole Martin family.

All those years ago Zacky Martin had been a small, tough, wrinkled man — wrinkled far before his time; now with real age and the long struggle against miners' tissick he had become tiny: a cashew nut instead of a brazil. Somehow Dwight kept him alive, mixing hot vapours for him to inhale at bad times, or potions of nux vomica and strychnine as a tonic for good ones.

This was a good one, and Ross, stooping into the small living room greeted them both and sat down. Mrs Zacky, who had delivered Demelza of Julia and helped at the births of Jeremy and Clowance, and who had had eight children of her own, had not shrivelled with the years: she was a stout, white-haired, bespectacled, flat-faced, rubicund, vigorous seventy-one. In the room, as it happened, were Gabby and Thomas, now both married and living at Marasanvose. They had been collecting driftwood (which Ross had stumbled over in the dark outside). The wrecks around the coast were breaking up and distributing their flotsam. Fortunately — from their point of view — old Vercoe, the Customs Officer at St Ann's, was known to be laid up with an ulcer on his leg.

Mrs Zacky said: "Well, I 'ad thought to go, an' then I thought not. Katie be very wilful; always 'ave been, will not be told. She've never even brought 'im round to see us. I mind 'im in church, o' course but he never come to no prayer meetings."

"She'm shamed of 'im," said Thomas. "That be the truth and no two ways o' looking 'pon it."

"I aren't so sartin he's so dead'n alive," said Gabby. "He's a treat wi' horses. An' I seen him quick 'nough 'pon times."

Zacky said: "Katie be wilful but she have her head screwed on. Maybe twill turn for the best."

210

There had been many improvements in the cottage since those early days: a good smooth planchen laid over the earth floor, and rugs on that; three comfortable upholstered chairs, a dark oak table, a mirror, a new fireplace; the ovens moved into the scullery. Zacky had prospered with his master. Ross had pressed him to move into a place less cramped for size, but as their family had grown and gone and his own active life became restricted Zacky had been less and less inclined to move.

Gabby relit his pipe. "I 'ear tell there's like to be trouble."

"Trouble?"

"Twas only a whisper I picked up but they d'say them lads that was always baiting Music, they d'plan to upset the wedden."

"Upset it? How?"

"Dunno. There's three or four lads, half a dozen girls, mischief bent, ye might say."

"What time is the wedding?"

"Nine o'clock," said Zacky. "After it they go back to work at Place House."

Mrs Zacky clicked her knitting needles. "Reckon I'll maybe go up to the church, if tis your wish, Cap'n Ross."

"Maybe I'll come along wi' ee, mam," said Gabby. "Tis slack time an' I can steal a hour."

"We'd best not be late leaving this eve," said Thomas. "There's a couple loads wood outside. If we can have the lend of your handcart, Father?"

"Anything of value come in?" Ross asked.

"Two spars o' good timber, sur, looks like black spruce or some such. Nought else you'd say of *value*."

"Think you they've come from the *Kinseale*?"

"They're small pieces, ten foot long, but there may be better on the morning tide."

"What time is high water? Ten or a little after? Well, it's worth keeping an eye open."

His mission accomplished, Ross led his horse home. He found Demelza seated before the fire reading to Henry; Bella and Cuby heads together over a piece of needlework; their latest cat, Hebe, licking a delicate back leg at Demelza's feet and Farquhar, nose in paws, drowsing in the steady candlelight.

When he came in all was commotion, movement, talk. Demelza went off immediately to see that supper should soon be served. She still hadn't learned the ability to delegate.

Against the probabilities, her relationship with Cuby had ripened into an easy friendship. There had been some moment of crisis, Ross sensed, soon after Cuby arrived, but that had passed. This peculiarly fraught, uneasy situation could so easily have failed because of the special tensions that operated within both women; and it was a testimony to Cuby, he thought, as well as to Demelza, that they spoke understandingly and affectionately to each other, considerate but not over-polite; they even sometimes differed on things, even shared a joke.

Next Monday Demelza was to go to Penryn to spend a few days with Clowance, and he knew she would try to persuade her to spend

Christmas with them. Ross's instinct was against it, but he did not utter a word. The second loss, coming so hard on the heels of the first, had left a raw edge that couldn't yet begin to heal. It was twisting the sword in the wound to attempt to keep up Christmas in any way whatever. If Clowance came she might find it hard to reconcile herself to the prospect of a new baby in the house and a sister-in-law about whom she still had resentful reservations. Dwight said he thought Cuby's child would be likely to be born in mid January. As soon as possible then Cuby would want to show the baby to her mother. That would be the time to press Clowance to come to Nampara. The longer the girls were kept apart while the first wounds healed, the better chance there was of their finding harmony and understanding.

★ ★ ★

Day came up about seven, with angry clouds which seemed to be a residue of some quarrel of the night. Ross took his spyglass to the window of his bedroom but the sea and beach were calm and unencumbered.

They breakfasted at 7.30, when Bella was full of some rhyme or jingle she had learned, supposing it to be the sounds a nightingale made when in full song. At eight Ross strolled out of the house as if going to Wheal Leisure, but instead walked up the Long Field and its promontory of rocks at Damsel Point which divided Hendrawna Beach from Nampara Cove.

The unbroken sand of Hendrawna Beach was a creamy white as the sun broke through, the placid sea, so wild a few days ago, turning gently over at its edge, playful wavelets bearing no visible cargo. The two Martin men had got the best last night.

He wondered how Katie's wedding would go. He hoped the village lads, who could be spiteful enough, would not interrupt the ceremony, or turn the evening into some sort of a noisy riot. He turned to go back to the house and then stopped to stare into Nampara Cove. By the freak of the tides practically all wreckage was washed up along the great beach, the cove scarcely ever gathered anything of note. Today the position was reversed. The cove was choked with wood.

He clambered down the side of the gorse-grown cliff and came out on the small beach, part sand, part pebbles, bisected by the Mellingey Stream. It took no time to recognize the wood as being good quality timber, more black spruce, red and yellow pine, oak and probably beech. There were also tar barrels and bales of rope and oakum floating around.

He touched nothing but began to limp quickly up the narrow green valley to the house. There were a half-dozen able-bodied men about the farm. They would be mainly in the fields by now. And Sephus Billing. Sephus Billing was this morning repairing the fowl house. He was a fair carpenter but his intellectual attainments would not have put Music to shame. And he was a member of the Billing clan who pullulated in

214

one of the larger cottages of Grambler village.

"Sephus!" Ross called as he came into the yard.

"Ais, sur?"

"There's a lot of good timber washing in in Nampara Cove. Go and tell the other men, I want them to stop work and go down to see what they can salvage."

A gleam lit up Sephus's dull eyes. He wiped his nose with the back of his hand. "Ais, sur, that I'll do." He put down his hammer. You never had to tell a Cornishman twice to down tools if there was booty to be had.

"And Sephus!" as he made for the gate.

"Sur?"

"When you have told the men you may go on to Grambler and tell your family of it. There should be a little bounty for all."

Ross walked to the gate and shut it after the fleeing man. With an ironical gaze he saw Sephus running in the direction of Cal Trevail, who was pulling carrots in the field beyond Demelza's garden. Soon there would be plenty of willing helpers. All Sephus had to do then was alert the village of Grambler.

★ ★ ★

Music and Katie went to church through a deserted village. No young men or girls waited by the wayside to douse them in liquid manure. They were married in an almost empty church, the only people present being Parson Odgers — and Mrs Odgers to remind him not to read the burial service in error — Jinny and Whitehead Scoble, Dr Enys, Mrs Zacky Martin, Char Nanfan, and a half-dozen old women who were too infirm to rush down for the pickings in Nampara Cove.

In the cove itself a fair element of chaos reigned, for the haul was bigger than it first seemed. A freak of tide had carried the cargo of the wrecked *Kinseale* out of Basset's Cove and deposited it several miles north. The way was narrow and people were trooping down and back, some with mules, some with wheelbarrows, some with boxes and sacks — anything that would carry or contain more than a pair of hands. Often they plunged into the water to grab some item of flotsam, often there were arguments, sometimes fights. Everybody came peaceable, but not everybody could contain their greed.

After appropriating for himself two or three nice lengths of wood, Ross left the villagers and his farm labourers to it. Let them have their fun while the going was good. It was doubtful if Vercoe would have hastened to put in an appearance if he had been well; as he was not, there was no risk at all. Cuby went with Demelza and Isabella-Rose to the edge of Damsel Point to watch. Just for half an hour there was the risk of the crowd getting out of control, but Ross said: "Let them be. There's no liquor. They'll have cleared everything as clean as a whistle by nightfall." And they had. Demelza wrinkled her nose at what she expected she would find trampled down in the muddy track of her special cove when she went to look in the morning.

Meantime Music and Katie had returned to their cottage, changed out of their Sunday clothes and walked to Place House to resume their duties. Katie was normally a living-in maid, but as master and mistress were away had been given permission to sleep out for a few nights. So in due course, which was late in the afternoon, they returned to the cottage together, tramping unspeaking through the windy dark. An hour before they returned, unknown to them, the lads and girls, tired out with a day of collecting timber and pieces of panelling and rope ends and paint brushes and a roll of calico and a man's jacket and other odds and ends, had bethought themselves of their old malice and decided — coming giggling out of a kiddley — that, well, they might just so well dump the pig shit as waste it, and they would be passing the cottage anyway on their way home. But they were thwarted by the startling and unexpected presence of Constable Vage, who happened to be taking a stroll in Grambler village at that time. It was the first time he had been in Grambler for a month. Ross, not being a magistrate, had no authority to call him out, but a discreet guinea sent over by Matthew Mark Martin had been enough, and he had whiled away the time talking and drinking with the Paynters until the drunken laughter of the lads alerted him afresh to Ross's request.

So the happy couple slept undisturbed, Katie in the upstairs room once occupied by the three

217

brothers, Music stretched out below in front of the dying fire.

He was perfectly, perfectly happy. She was his wife. She was upstairs in his house, along of him.

If it never came to no more than that, he would be content. If it someday came to the as-yet-unthinkable he would be enraptured. But for the time being he was perfectly, blissfully satisfied with the simple fact that they were wed. Beyond that his patience stretched away into the illimitable distance.

2

LADY HARRIET WARLEGGAN was brought to bed on the evening of Wednesday, the 12th December, and her labour continued into the morning of the 13th.

Things had not been easy between Harriet and George. Harriet was tetchy all the time, plagued by thoughts of the accident and made more angry by George's reactions to it. He seemed to take it as a breach of convention, even an insult to himself, that his wife and this upstart he disliked so much and whom Harriet well knew he disliked so much, who had been guilty of highway robbery against him — that they should have been defiantly and openly riding together; and that she had put their son at risk for the sake of some stupid and high-spirited gallop across hunting country . . . It never quite emerged whether Harriet had challenged Stephen or Stephen Harriet, but there had been some sort of competitiveness involved, of that George was sure. And he was not at all certain that there had not been some sexual undertones.

Indeed he had nurtured a number of suspicions ever since Harriet had virtually blackmailed him into withdrawing his bankruptcy notice. Her overt reason, because Clowance had rescued her dog, had never convinced George.

Being a man who disliked dogs and only tolerated hounds because they contributed to a national sport, he was unable to fathom the feelings of a woman who felt as Harriet did. Stephen was a personable man — if you liked the braggart type — and he had made a fuss of Harriet. She clearly had a soft spot for him, and had blown up her obligation to Clowance to hide her real feelings. The fact that they had gone riding — galloping! — together was proof enough that something had been afoot.

Well, serve them both right if he'd broken his damned back. It was a miracle that she hadn't fallen too and taken with her his hopes of an heir.

George had mixed feelings about Stephen's death. It was good riddance, of course, and it wiped the slate clean. All the same it would have been better if he could have somehow been arrested for the crime he had committed and ended his life dangling from a noose. Now he had escaped. And with him had gone any hope there might have been of tracking down his two accomplices. The chapter was over and done with. Only Clowance was left on whom he might vent his spleen.

But that George had no intention of doing. Ross Poldark was winged by the loss of his eldest son. His eldest daughter — yes, there was another one; that one with the raucous voice — seemed bent on continuing to live in Penryn for the time being; and George thought he might well make some gesture to befriend her. Although she was a Poldark with her share of

Poldark arrogance, he had always been attracted by her, ever since they had first met at Trenwith when she had wandered barefoot into the great hall blatantly trespassing. Indeed it might be said that it was his encounter with the fresh young Clowance, carrying her bouquet of stolen foxgloves, which had first aroused him to recover his appreciation of women in general, a process which had led to his courtship of Lady Harriet Carter and their eventual marriage.

Of course, apart from a salacious look or two, George had not the least serious sexual intent towards the young widow; but if he did find a way of befriending her it would, he thought, make his old rival irritable and suspicious and might even raise a tremor of annoyance and jealousy in his own wife.

During the period of waiting that dark December night George paced the wide drawing-room of Cardew and nursed his hopes and his grievances and listened for noises from upstairs. His latest grievance was but an hour old. When Dr Charteris had arrived to join Dr Behenna, who was already in attendance, George had gone into the bedroom with them for a moment or two. There had been sweat on his wife's brow, and the midwife was holding her hand. Looking up and seeing him, Harriet had said between her teeth: "Get out of my sight!"

He had at once retreated, fuming at her rudeness. Very well, it was a painful business and women suffered a great deal and sometimes they were driven to unwarranted comment; and of course as a woman of blue blood Harriet was accustomed to expressing herself coarsely; but it was inexcusable for her to address him thus in front of both surgeons and the midwife! Over the years he had become a man of whom all those with whom he mixed were wary and respectful; even a man like Behenna, who was used to riding roughshod over his patients, deferred to Sir George. Only his wife, his lady wife, could ever have dared to speak to him in this way, and he felt insulted and demeaned by her.

He passed little Ursula's bedroom. Little Ursula was not there, being at school, and was no longer little, being a hefty, heavy-legged, tight-busted girl of sixteen. It had been her birthday last Sunday, and they had given her a party despite the imminence of her step-mother's 'time'. A select group, carefully chosen from among the best in the county; some had stayed overnight because of the distances involved. A pity Ursula was not a more becoming girl, with the blonde hair, frailty and long slender legs of her mother. Instead she was like her paternal grandmother in looks, and sadly looks counted for so much in a girl. She was a chip off the old Warleggan block. But fortunately not at all like her maternal grandmother in a practical or sagacious sense. George's mother, born a miller's daughter with simple beliefs and a country understanding, had never quite moved into the world of opulence her husband had made for her, had always preferred making jam and baking bread to riding in a carriage with two postilions or entertaining on a grand scale.

Such matters would not be likely to worry

Ursula. If not intellectual — and who wanted her to be? — she was sharply intelligent and fascinated by commerce and money. An ideal child from George's point of view, if only she had been a son. And, being a girl, it were better had she been more prepossessing.

All the same, he thought, it would really only be a matter of arrangement when the time came. An heiress would have plenty of suitors. It would be a question of his picking the right one; they'd all fall over themselves.

It did not occur to him to recall that the one chink in his own personal chain-armour of self-help had been his weakness for a pretty face. Yet he expected that Ursula would find the ideal husband chiefly on the strength of an enormous dowry, just as he had expected his son to match with a Trevanion in order to secure the land and the castle. *And* there had certainly been no lack of looks on the Trevanion side! Instead Valentine had maliciously and wantonly married a pretty widow ten years older than himself without his father's knowledge or consent. George had made sure that not a penny of his money or property should ever go to Valentine. He had written him out of his will and out of his life.

Now, upstairs at this moment, another life was beginning and if, pray God, it was a son he could begin to reshape his plans all over again. Indeed he had already begun to reshape them. The boy should be called Nicholas after his father. Then he could be called anything Harriet fancied, some favourite family name of her own. Perhaps Thomas, after the first

223

Duke. Nicholas Thomas Osborne Warleggan, that would do well enough.

The house was dark and cold at 2.15 on a December morning. Fires roared upstairs, especially in The Room, and fires roared downstairs, but the house was still draughty; if you crouched within the periphery of one of the fires it was warm enough, even scorching. But if you were too tensed up to remain in one position for any length of time you quickly became aware of the draughts and the dark. Even the candles guttered.

It was a time of night when spirits were low and human nature at its lowest ebb. As he paced about, George recollected that when he had last been in this situation, in December '99, both his own parents had been alive and both Elizabeth's. Now all were gone. Sixteen years spanned so much of his own life, which was fast slipping away. He would soon be fifty-seven. Many men died at such an age. He was filled with a sense of the impermanence of life, with a premonition of disaster. Trenwith was no longer his, had gone back to the Poldarks. This great house which he had bought and repaired and refurnished and extended a quarter of a century ago was now the centre of his life. How long would it remain in Warleggan hands after he was gone? The renegade Valentine was established on the north coast with his own rich widow and his two step-daughters. Ursula might marry and live here. Perhaps, who knew, if he found the right sort of husband for her, he could persuade the young man for a consideration to take not only the Warleggan daughter but the Warleggan name.

But all that would be unnecessary if Harriet tonight produced a healthy son. A Warleggan who could come into everything he did not set expressly aside for Ursula, and who would, in addition to being the son of Sir George Warleggan, be also a grandson of the Duke of Leeds! It was a dazzling prospect. True, by the time he was eighteen he, George, would be seventy-five. But — rejecting the dark thoughts of a moment ago — he recalled that the Warleggans were a long-lived family; both his parents had been around eighty, and old Uncle Cary at seventy-six showed no signs at all of closing his last ledger.

Tock-tock went the clock in the hall. It wanted twenty minutes to three. This damned waiting seemed worse even than last time. Elizabeth had never been in labour long. That had never been the trouble. Harriet of course was thirty-four. It was late for a first child. How old had Elizabeth been when she bore Ursula? He could not remember. Thirty-five, was it? But Ursula had been her third.

The candles bobbed and ducked like courtiers. It was a fine night but windy, a big cold empty night with a scattering of stars among the clouds. Half his staff was abed, but the other half was alert for the slightest pull of a bell. At the moment Nankivell was making up the fires.

"Sur, can I get you something?"

"No." He had drunk enough brandy, and

225

there was a half-glass unfinished on the end of the mantelshelf.

He sat down at his desk, took some papers out of a drawer and irritably pulled a candelabrum nearer so that he could see. It was on a matter to do with his pocket borough of St Michael. Years ago he had reduced the number of voters in the borough from forty to thirty by the simple but drastic expedient of moving ten of them out of their derelict cottages and rehousing them two miles away in much better property which he had had restored especially to receive them. They could not plead hardship, since their new housing was much better than the old; but they were deprived of their sinecure living by no longer having to be bribed to vote. Their vote was gone, and so was their means of sustenance. As George had dryly observed at the time, some of them might even have to *work*. Since then gradually over the years the remaining number had been reduced to twenty-five, of whom six were members of one family. Mr Tankard, George's legal steward, had called in at the beginning of the month to say that this family was now applying for a loan of three hundred pounds. It was supposed to be to erect a bakery, but everyone knew it was intended to tide them over until the next election, when they would expect the loan to be conveniently forgotten. George had no intention of submitting to this blackmail, in spite of the advice of his friend Sir Christopher Hawkins that he should do so. Hawkins had said: "It is the price you pay, my friend. Think nothing of it. Think rather of the benefits of having two members in the House to do your bidding." But George would have none of it. He was not to be held to ransom by a festering family of down-at-heel good-for-nothings, and he was determined to make them pay for their insolence. He felt very strongly about it, and this was why he had dragged out the correspondence, with Tankard's notes, tonight. If anything would take his mind off events upstairs . . .

He pored over it for a minute or so, fumbling for his glasses and feeling the stirrings of old anger; but then he flung the papers down and got to his feet. Even this —

And then he heard a sound, it was a terrible sound, like a wail, like a howl, almost more animal than human. Sweat broke out on him. Supposing Harriet were to die. That would not matter quite so much if the boy lived. But they might *both* die. George found himself confronting a great loneliness which opened up before him like a mining adit. In spite of Harriet's infuriating habits she was a remarkable personality, whose very abrasiveness he would bitterly miss. And if the child were to go . . .

He strode out into the hall and stopped to listen. All was silent now. A log of wood crashed in the hearth and the resultant flames lit up the sombre room where many times there had been so much gaiety and light. Where Harriet and Valentine had organized that great party to celebrate Napoleon's retreat from Moscow; where only a few days ago Ursula's friends —

The same sound again but more muffled. He

took out a handkerchief and mopped his brow, started up the stairs toward the sound, then stopped, puzzled, angry, horrified, his heart thumping. A groom crossed the hall, seemed to be coming this way.

"Smallwood!"

"Sur?"

"Where are you going?"

"Up the stairs, sur, beggin' your permission. Lady Harriet said as I was — "

"Never mind what she said, you've no damned business above stairs."

"No, sur. It was just that she did say I was to look to — "

That terrible sound again, loud now. George's hair prickled.

"Get out!" he snarled.

"Yes, sur. I just had the thought that the dogs making that noise might be disturbing to her ladyship — "

"Dogs? What dogs?"

"Castor and Pollux, sur. Her ladyship give me orders that they was to be lodged in the blue bedroom while she was — while she was in labour, as you might say. Her ladyship didn't wish for them to be roaming the 'ouse while she was poorly and she thought they'd be best out of your — out of the way. I was to lock them in the blue bedroom and see they was kept fed and watered. That is why I was venturing — "

"That noise, that howling," George said. "It was the dogs howling?"

"Yes, sur. I thought I'd just go see — "

"Go and see to them!" George shouted. "Stop

228

their damned mouths, stop their throats even if you have to cut them! Give them poison so long as you keep them *quiet!*"

"Yes, sur." In fright Smallwood slid past his master and rushed stumbling up the rest of the stairs, then with anxious backward glances retreated down the passage towards the blue bedroom.

George went back slowly down, breathing out rage and relief, and more indignation with every breath. An outrageous thing to happen! Putting the dogs in a bedroom! He'd wondered where they had gone to — how typical of Harriet's arrogance and thoughtlessness for him! He would tell her exactly how he viewed such a ridiculous act. Almighty God, for a moment — for some minutes — he had thought, he had feared . . .

A step behind him.

He swung round. Dr Behenna. Sleeves rolled up. Black waistcoat with gold chain. Grey hair *en brosse*. A silly look on his face.

"Well?"

"I am happy to tell you that her ladyship has been safely delivered of twins."

"*What* d'you say?"

"I had thought this likely since before ten o'clock last evening, but did not wish to raise your hopes. Mother and babies are all doing well. There have been no complications. My sincere congratulations, Sir George."

George stared at the doctor with astonishment and such a concentration of anxiety and anger as to disconcert him.

"The second child is slightly smaller but in excellent condition," Behenna hastened on. "She was born half an hour after her sister."

"*Sister?*" said George. "You mean . . . ?"

"You have two fine daughters, Sir George. I am sure you will be vastly proud of them. Lady Harriet has been very brave, and I will give her a further opiate as soon as you have seen them."

3

DEMELZA rode back on the 14th from visiting Clowance again. Cuby was out walking on the beach with Isabella-Rose, Henry was with Mrs Kemp. Demelza found Ross in the garden.

"Well," she said, "I did not know you knew one plant from another. I hope you have not been digging up my new bulbs."

"Cuby saw to that," Ross said, kissing her. "I believe since she brought them she has been watching every day for them to come up."

Demelza knelt and stirred the soil with her finger. "These are late tulips, she says. They do not flower until May."

Ross crouched beside her. "Clowance?"

"Better. Eating at last. She has lost a lot of weight. I do not think she will come home for Christmas, Ross."

"Ah."

"She said to me: 'Mama I will come — of course I will come with pleasure if you wish me to, if you wish this Christmas specially to have all your family round you,' she said. 'But if it were my own choice I would, I believe, better prefer to remain here with Verity. I do not know quite how to explain it,' she said, 'but it is certain that this Christmas cannot be a Christmas like last year or any other year we have ever known. So I think it would affect me less if I could look

231

on it as just the 25th of December, another day of the month,' she said, 'like any other day of any month and *try* to forget it is happening.'"

Ross straightened up, aware that his ankle did not like a crouching position. He had had reservations about Clowance coming back too soon for another and altogether particular reason — that is, that in her first bereavement she might see too much of Ben Carter. It was a strange perception for him, and more worthy of Demelza. But under no circumstances would he mention such a feeling to her.

"Shall you mind so much?"

"Not if she is with Verity."

"How is she dealing with the business?"

"Both ships were out. The boy, this nephew of his, was away in the *Adolphus*, which was being captained by a man called Carter. The *Lady Clowance* was sailing for the Thames with a cargo of china clay. At home, in the port, a strange little man called Hodge is helping her. He is almost horrid to look at, but she seems to trust him. He can read and write and do accounts. And the Naval Bank is also helping: Stephen has left quite a lot of money, it seems, all from this privateering adventure."

"I'll go over myself next week; spend a night or two."

The wind was tugging at Demelza's hat. She put a hand up to it.

"She has changed, Ross. I — I think she has been deeply injured — of course by her bereavement, of course, but I suspicion something more than that. It is as if she no

232

longer has confidence in her own judgement — as if she is confused as well as desperately heart-sad. I cannot make it out . . . She is harder than she used to be. I feel she will need careful handling — specially careful handling."

"By us?"

"I hope so. And by life . . . "

Ross frowned out at the sea.

"Even with the war over," he said, "the ships should fetch a good price. If, then, she doesn't want to make her home permanently with us she could travel. She has no family and is still so young . . . It's a grim travesty that we should find ourselves with two young widows on our hands."

"I do not know that she wishes to sell the ships — at least for the time being. She seems to feel Stephen would have wanted her to keep them. I think they would give her a sense of independence greater than she would have just with the money they would fetch. Also she wants to look after Stephen's nephew, for a few months at least. She says he is utterly lost."

"She must have time to adjust herself. It will take months, perhaps years. Of course there will be other men in the world. But not too soon."

"Do you know what she said to me? It was the strangest thing!"

"What?"

"We were just talking, just talking, and I said like you said, that she was so young, she had all her life ahead of her. I'd never've dreamed of saying anything about her marrying again. 'Twould have been premature and improper and impertinent. But she must've read my thoughts, or 'twas in the air in some strange way." Demelza took off her hat and let the wind ruffle her hair. "She said: 'I married once for love, Mama. If I ever come to marry again,' she said, 'it will not be for love, it will be for wealth or position.'"

Ross was silent.

Demelza said: "Does that not surprise you?"

"It astounds me. You are right to say she has changed. But it means . . . "

"It surely means that her marriage was not altogether successful."

"A lot of marriages are not altogether successful. Look around. But it is sad if she discovered it so early. And it is the bitterest thing for *her* to say."

"Yet she clearly loved Stephen. I cannot fathom it."

Ross took her hat from her and they walked towards the house.

Demelza said: "Lady Harriet has had twins, I hear. All are well. They are both girls."

"George will be beside himself with annoyance," said Ross, not without satisfaction.

"I s'pose he laid great store by having another son. There has been no reconciliation between him and Valentine, has there?"

"Nor ever like to be," said Ross.

Demelza glanced up at him sharply as they went in. "Valentine called here once while I was away?"

"Who told you?"

"Mrs Kemp just mentioned it."

"It was in October. He did not come in. We walked down from Grace together and talked for a few minutes."

"Did he say they could never be reconciled?"

"He gave me that impression."

"Never is a long time. I think I rather hope they will . . . Did he want anything when he came?"

"It was just to say goodbye before they left for Cambridge."

Demelza thought this one through. "Why did you say they would never be reconciled?"

"A feeling I have."

"Something he said."

"Just a feeling I have."

She was very perceptive of nuances in Ross's voice, but after a moment she decided she should not pursue it.

"I hear Valentine and Selina will not be home for Christmas."

"Oh?"

"Ben told me. They are going to spend the Christmas vacation in London with her two daughters. Katie has heard and she told her mother."

"No hint of Ben and Katie coming together again?"

"Not yet. But have you met Music recent? He is quite an improved man."

"Some people marry and it changes their personalities, it seems. Others marry and it makes not the slightest difference."

"How do you think it affected us?" Demelza asked.

"We re-made each other after the other's image."

"That's a little complicated for my small mind, but I hope I know what you mean."

They went in. He said: "So we shall be a reduced company in this area for Christmas. Geoffrey Charles and Amadora and Joanna are in Paris. Drake and Morwenna and Loveday will, I am sure, return to Looe, for he has problems at the yard. So there will be just Dwight and Caroline and the girls and a smattering of Trenegloses and Kellows."

"Perhaps Clowance is right and, just for this year, we should pretend it isn't happening." At the parlour door Demelza exclaimed on seeing a vase of flowers: carnations, picotees and lace pinks. "Judas! Where did they come from?"

"The de Dunstanvilles sent them over. They only came this morning."

"That is so kind of them, Ross! That is kind." Once in a while Demelza's eyes would fill with tears unnecessarily.

"They have been put in water just as they came. Cuby said, should she arrange them, but I said I thought you would want to do it. And hot-house grapes!"

"I will write. Or *you* will write. Yes, a bigger vase, don't you think? And I can gather some ferns and ivy to go with them. There's time before dark."

"Just time."

At the door she stopped, wiped her eyes with an inelegant hand. "We cannot ignore Christmas altogether. There is little Henry. And Bella. And

236

Sophie and Meliora, who will come over. And Cuby — who may be deeply sad but has a child within her. We shall somehow have to make — a sort of, what do you call it?"

"Compromise?"

"Yes. How you read my thoughts — "

"Long association — "

"Compromise, that is what it must be. No big celebration. But quiet celebration. After all it is to commemorate the birth of Christ."

Ross smiled at her, for her eyes had briefly lit up in a way he had not seen for some time.

"Just so," he said. "Just so."

★ ★ ★

He went to Penryn the following Tuesday, leaving before dawn and arriving at midday. He had a meal with Clowance and then they rowed down the creek to Falmouth and walked up to Pendennis Castle, where many years ago he had stayed with Governor Melville discussing defence matters. Just before the miners' riots. There had been a number of smaller outbreaks of violence since, but none with that tragic ending.

He did not call this time, but they turned and walked back down the gorse-grown hill towards the town. Clowance remarked that her father's ankle seemed much better; he replied that if it got bad again he would try three months' internment to improve it. All through his visit they had talked long and amiably on many subjects, including details of Jeremy's death and the consequences of Stephen's. They took supper together and he slept there and left to return home the following morning; he would dine at the Fox & Grapes, near St Day, on the way home.

That night Clowance spent with Verity. Andrew junior was ashore until Christmas Eve when he sailed again for New York, but this evening with Tamsin and her brother was attending a small soirée and dance given by one of the other packet captains. Clowance had been invited but had declined. Andrew senior, having had a minor recurrence of his heart affection, had gone to bed.

Clowance said: "D'you know, it is quite unusual, but since I — since I lost Stephen I have had more single conversations with my mother and father than I can ever remember in my life before. Before, of course, I met them *constantly* in and out of the house. But never in such a concentrated way, if you take my meaning. Most often if it was anything important the three of us would meet together. You must know the — the triviality of daily life. Now we have talked so much, in a different way."

"Your father looked better," Verity said.

"Yes, he was, he was. They both looked so dreadful when I saw them first — after Jeremy. But life has to go on." Clowance smiled wryly. "Even for me."

"More than ever for you," Verity said.

"Yes, I suppose. But at present I'm in limbo.

238

I don't really want to make any decisions at all if I haven't got to."

"Give yourself a year, my dear. Stephen has left you money enough."

"Do you know I grieve so much that he was not able to *enjoy* the good fortune. All his life he had been poor — grindingly poor." Clowance hesitated. "At least, I think so."

"What do you mean?"

"I mean that just before he died I discovered an important inaccuracy in something he had told me. And that — and that calls into question some of the other things he told me." Clowance got up, picked up a magazine, riffled through the pages. "No, I think I am being unfair. What he told me that was untrue was something important to — to our marriage. I do not believe he would have told me circumstantial stories of his poverty if they had not happened."

Verity looked up at her tall young cousin. Demelza had been right: the ordeal Clowance had been through, her loss of weight, had aged her but improved her looks.

Clowance said: "Although I can talk to Papa freely about most things — and I do! — I cannot really talk to him about Stephen, for I do not think he ever altogether cared for Stephen. They were such *opposite* characters, yet in some ways rather alike."

"Alike? I would not — I don't think I would . . . "

"Well, they were both very strong, weren't they — physically strong, masculine, courageous, stop-at-nothing sort of men . . . After that,

239

no . . . they were not really alike. I wonder why I said that? Perhaps I am trying to make reasonable what to some people was unreasonable, which was my love for Stephen."

Verity got up to put some coal on the fire.

"Let me do that." Clowance moved quickly to the fire. Verity saw a tear drop on the coal.

"I am sure your father understands what you felt."

"Oh, he understands that I loved Stephen. But not why. You see one does not *choose*. I have said this to Mama — oh a year ago, but it comes home even more truly now. One loves a person — feels deeply drawn to love him, and no one else will do. And because you love him you suppose he has all the virtues which he does not have. So one expects more than one gets, and that is wrong . . . I do not believe I am making sense, Verity. It is just helpful to talk to you."

"Is it Jason who is bothering you?"

"Jason? Oh no. No, not really. You know he is Stephen's son by an earlier marriage?"

"I did not know. Your mother wondered."

"Did she? Mama has a dangerous intuition. But even her intuition, I believe, will not perceive all that I have in my heart to tell her if I would. But I will not. Nor will I tell you, dear cousin, for I believe it is best buried with Stephen."

Clowance busied herself with the fire; Verity picked up her embroidery but did not take out the needle.

In a calmer voice Clowance said: "There was

one thing I did not *dare* tell Papa. It happened on Monday. I had a visitor. You will never guess. It was Sir George Warleggan."

Verity stared at her. "George?"

"He came with two grooms. I heard the clattering of horses and looked up the street and saw him just dismounted. As he walked down, with one of the other men — I think his name is Nankivell — I was quite terrified. I thought he was going to arrest me!"

"What did he want?"

"Well, when I opened the door he just took off his hat and gave me good-day; I could hardly find the words to speak so I stood aside and he came in. He is not nearly so tall as Papa, but he takes up a deal of room in a small parlour! I said would he sit down and he said no doubt I might be a trifle surprised at his visit, but he just was passing through Penryn and it occurred to him to call to see if he could help me in any way. There had been some ill-feeling, he said, between him and my husband, but now that Stephen was so unfortunately gone he would like to remind me of the goodwill that existed between himself and Lady Harriet and me, and if he could be of assistance to me in my widowhood, either in a social or a financial sense, he would ask me to name it!"

Verity did not speak. She had thirty years of memories of George, most of them bad; but she felt she need not add them to Clowance's own.

"Dear cousin, I was — flabbergasted! I have not seen Harriet since the accident; for Stephen had quarrelled with her for some reason and would speak not a single good word of her. I suppose I too felt that day she had behaved not well, but . . . She wrote to us when Stephen was ill and then again to me after he died, but I had not replied. Now George coming like this . . . " Clowance wrinkled her forehead. "I thanked him and said I thought I was engaging myself well enough. He said he understood Stephen had left a little money, but if I should be in need of legal advice he would be happy to have it provided for me. And when a due time of mourning had been observed I should be welcome again at the hunt or some other occasion if I should feel the want of company. It was all very gracious, I assure you."

"George can be gracious enough — and generous enough — when he chooses. But usually with a reason."

"Soon after that he left, having refused a glass of canary, which was all I had in the place. I have wondered since why he came. Ever since I met him that first time five years ago I believe he has had a very small taking for me. But still . . . "

"George has a weak spot for a few women. I remember particularly — " Verity stopped. "For fair women especially . . . Though that is contradicted by his second marriage, is it not."

"That is another strange thing!" Clowance said. "I offered my congratulations, saying I knew how happy he must be at the birth of his baby daughters, and he glanced at me as if he thought I was sarcastic, or deriding him in some way."

"A daughter for George," Verity said, "is near to a catastrophe."

There was silence for a while.

Clowance said: "I think I should like a cup of chocolate. Shall I make you some?"

"It would be nice. But pull the bell. Anna is up till ten."

Clowance pulled the bell. Thoughtfully she rearranged her hair with both hands.

"Papa thinks Cuby's child will be a boy."

"Why?"

"He says something about the law of averages. Geoffrey Charles had a girl. Your step-son has just had a girl. Now George and Harriet's two! I do not know if averages work in such things."

"I do not suppose it matters very much, does it? Either will be welcome."

"It matters about Papa's title, that is all."

Anna came in and Verity ordered the chocolate.

★ ★ ★

Demelza said: "Tell me, Caroline, I have intended to have asked you before; what would you say, how would you feel if either of your daughters wished, wanted to become an actress or a professional singer, like?"

Caroline raised her eyebrows. "I do not believe either of 'em has sufficient talent to shine even in amateur theatricals. Why?"

"I have a special reason for asking, which I suppose you will guess refers to Bella."

"She certainly has a remarkable voice — even

243

though her father affects not to appreciate it. But has she shown some sudden ambition?"

"She was quite overcome with the theatre we took her to in London. I have never seen her so enchanted. But there is another reason. While we were in Paris we met a young English lieutenant who must have put ideas in her head . . . Oh, it is all over and done with now, but it was some startling how it happened — and to a girl as young as she is!"

So it came out: the jolly camaraderie, the avuncular courtship, and then the sudden visit and the serious proposal.

Caroline listened in silence, playing with the ears of Horace the Third.

"What does Ross think of this?"

"I haven't told him. To begin I was too — too desolate to think of anything but Jeremy. And then came the news that Christopher Havergal had been cruelly maimed. Then it was all struck out of my mind when I knew nothing would come of it. But I often thought to ask you . . . "

"Did Bella know of his proposal?"

"Oh yes. And of course when news came of his wounding she was even more totally despondent: first for Jeremy and then for Christopher. But now more recently she has recovered much of her bounce and good spirits, so perhaps she will forget all about it. But I only wonder if it has not left an impression on her mind which will show in a year or two. And I wondered . . . "

"You wondered?"

"What you would say if you were in my place

if next year or the year after Bella said she wished to — to become a singer or an actress for — for money. How would you feel if it were Sophie, for instance?"

Caroline let Horace to the floor with a plop. He grunted a protest.

"You will have to tell Ross sometime, and it will greatly depend on what he feels, will it not. For my part I would look on the prospect with a degree of doubt. Actors and singers are not of any social standing. Some lead a disorganized life and are thoroughly disreputable. Others are respectable but are not generally respected. A few singers, and great actresses like Siddons, they are different; but it will be very few . . . Of course another way to become highly regarded is to become the mistress of one of the Royal Princes. But even then, from reports, it does not seem to lead to a settled or comfortable life."

Demelza shifted in her chair. "Christopher was a very taking young man; but in truth it was perhaps all too trivial, too light-hearted to be taken serious. It was unthinkable anyway. But I am greatly relieved that Bella appears to have recovered from it altogether."

Caroline said: "It shows how easily the young forget."

4

"SWEET, sweet, jug, jug, water bubble, pipe rattle," sang Isabella-Rose. "Bell pipe, scroty, skeg, skeg, swat, swaty, whitlow, whitlow, whitlow . . . Mama, do you hear me? That is what the nightingale sings. If we could but put it to music!"

Demelza had come into the library. Cuby was at the piano, Bella half dancing beside it.

Cuby said: "It is almost nice enough as you say it."

"But Mama is good at finding little tunes; she does not play so well but she has a knack of finding funny little tunes!"

It was Christmas Eve; outside a mild grey day, inside more fires than were strictly necessary, lit to enliven the house. The church choir were coming tonight; tomorrow they were all summoned to Killewarren, where the Enyses had ordered a boar's head for dinner. Aside from the Poldarks, the servants in Nampara had worked their way into a festive mood. Mr Jeremy had been lost, and everyone grieved for him and for Miss Clowance, also widowed. But it did not prevent jollity sneaking in, a condition that Christmas traditionally induced. There were sniggers and flutters and cat-calls. While the Poldarks were out tomorrow there would be a feast in the old kitchen — where Jud and Prudie had once reigned — and gracious knew what noise there would be. Ross wondered how many of his helpers he would find sober when they returned. And little cared.

Demelza was induced to sit at the piano in Cuby's place and Bella intoned over and over the jingle she had garnered from some old woman. "Sweet, sweet, jug, jug, water bubble, pipe rattle." So it went on while Demelza tried to find chords to fit it. "Bell pipe, scroty, skeg, skeg, swat, swaty, whitlow, whitlow, whitlow." Slowly a little tune came out. Bella crowed with delight, and Cuby and Demelza laughed together.

On this scene came Henry, and Bella gathered him up while Demelza played some of the old carols she knew so well.

The library was decorated with holly and ivy and ferns and a few early primroses, as was the parlour. Yesterday they had all been over to Sawle Church helping to decorate that too. Although flowers were scarce, some had come from Place House and from Killewarren. Neither Nampara nor Trenwith had a conservatory, and the Tregneloses were committed to St Ermyn's, Marasanvose. Before going to Killewarren tomorrow they would all go to Sawle Church, where Mr Clarence Odgers would read prayers and preach. For this great occasion of Christmas all the servants from Nampara would attend as well.

Dwight and Caroline had promised to be there, even though Dwight pointed out that the 25th December had been a day of festival in England long before its conversion to Christianity.

247

Christmas Eve passed peacefully enough, the dark coming early because of the gloom of cloud. At seven Cuby said she did not feel well and retired to bed early. But she heard the choir come, and got up and sat by the window listening. The choir, fourteen strong, sang the Dilly Song.

Come and I will sing you.
What will you sing O?
I will sing One O.
What is your One O?

Twelve are the Twelve Apostles
'Leven are the 'leven will go to Heaven
Ten are the Ten Commandments
Nine is the moonshine bright and clear
Eight are the Eight Archangels
Seven are the Seven Stars in the sky
Six the Cheerful Waiter
Five is the Ferryman in the boat
Four are the Gospel Praychers
Three of them are strangers
Two of them are Lilly-white babes
Clothed all in green-o
One of them is all alone and ever shall
remain so.

They also sang 'Noël' and 'Joseph Was An Old Man'.

Afterwards they trooped into the parlour and took mince tarts and ginger wine. Music and Katie were of the party, though Music would now only sing tenor and Katie could hardly sing at all. They stood together through it all with an air of indestructibility.

On Christmas Day Cuby was well again, so the planned programme went ahead. Dawn broke misty wet, but towards midday the lips of the sky opened and a drier breath came. All the same there had just been enough rain in the night to make the cobbles greasy, the yard steamy with animals, the tracks slippery with mud. Both mining engines still worked; it was too expensive to shut them down for a single day. In the quiet air their thump and beat became more noticeable.

At church Mr Odgers wore his best cassock which he kept for special occasions, it being plum purple with brass buttons, very tight now, for he had worn it first at his marriage fifty-one years ago. It indicated no doctrinal or ecclesiastical order, for he belonged to none. That morning he was at his best and got through the service with only two mistakes.

The psalm was part of 22, beginning at verse 11. "Be not far from me; for trouble is near; for there is none to help." When it came to verse 20, "Deliver my soul from the sword; my darling from the power of the dog," Demelza put her hand quietly into Ross's. His hand closed on hers.

After it was over they rode on to Killewarren, a few faint sun-born shadows preceding them on the way.

They had bought Caroline a piece of fine French lace, Dwight a neckerchief, and silk pinafores for the girls; the Enyses had a pair of wine goblets for Demelza, riding gloves for Ross, a finely crocheted child's bonnet for Cuby, a book of songs for Bella, a toy horse for Harry that however much you pushed it over would always swing upright again.

Because of the children they dined early, and laughed a good deal and ate consumedly and drank good wine and generally made merry, though there was ice underneath, ice that clung round the heart. Shut out thoughts of other Christmases, other shadows on the wall. This was an evil year; there would be others that must be better. Life was to be lived — it had to go on. Chiefly for the sake of the young, but even for themselves, it must go on. And the day was fine and mild and the fire crackled, and food and drink and love and companionship were around them. Do not think of Jeremy lying in the cold Flanders clay.

Darkness fell and candles were brought and the fires remade, and the two Enys girls sang a duet with Cuby at the piano, and Bella gave a little recital of her new nightingale song.

Sweet, sweet, jug, jug
Water bubble, pipe rattle
Bell pipe, scroty, skeg, skeg,
Swat, swaty, whitlow, whitlow, whitlow.

Her mother did her best to remember the chords she had made up that morning, and somehow it came out as a pleasant little ditty.

By 6.30 Henry was fretful, so Demelza, arousing huge protests from the girls, said they must go. They were away by seven, a small clip-clopping cavalcade, led by Ross, whose old Colley was as surefooted as they came and knew the way blindfold. Bone accompanied them carrying a lantern, though everyone assured Dwight it was not necessary.

A very dark night, unlit by moon or stars, and with a faint freckle of rain again borne on the tired breeze. Demelza carried Henry ahead of her, but as his head drooped in sleep he was transferred to Ross who, riding astride, could keep a firmer grip of him. A quiet ride now, everyone silent after the chatter of the day. In the distance the lights of Nampara already showed up, misting, haloed through the dark. As they clopped down the lane, overgrown with wind-crouching trees, Ross thought how little had changed here from the time he had ridden this way in the autumn of 1783 — thirty-two years ago — returning from the American War to find his father dead and Nampara a stinking shambles with Jud and Prudie in a drunken stupor in his father's old box bed.

They crossed the bridge and dismounted outside the front door. He took Demelza in his arms, then Cuby.

As she slipped close to him Cuby whispered: "I'm sorry. I think I am beginning my pains."

★ ★ ★

It was ten days earlier than anyone had supposed, but Ross said, as the lantern carrier was about to turn away:

"Bone."

"Sur?"

"I am very sorry, but I think my daughter-in-law is unwell. If you would trouble your master to come."

Cuby went upstairs and undressed at once. It was immediately clear to Demelza that she was not mistaken. Ross went into the kitchen and found less confusion than he had expected. Sephus Billing was under the table and Ern Lobb snoring in his chair, but the rest came to their feet as he walked in.

He smiled: "You have all dined well? I can see you have."

There was a relieved laugh. "Ais, sur."

"Sure 'nough."

"'Andsome, 'andsome, sur."

He looked at Matthew Mark Martin. "I must ask a service of you. Mrs Jeremy is taken with her pains. It is a little premature, but I have sent for Dr Enys. Will you ride to The Bounders' Arms and fetch Mrs Hartnell?"

"Right away, sur."

Since Emma had moved into The Bounders' Arms with her husband and two children, she had been encouraged by Dr Enys to take over from the elderly Mrs Higgins as midwife to the more respectable houses. It was not unremarked that this 'light' girl (daughter of the rascally Tholly Tregirls), who had at one time been considered to have too blemished a reputation to wed the Wesleyan, Sam Carne, should now in early middle life be looked on as reputable and reliable.

Demelza sat with Cuby to begin, regretting that, not expecting the baby until January, they had let Mrs Kemp take a holiday now, and that Clemency was not expected for another week. She felt nervous and ill-at-ease with this pretty small elegant young woman who was about to bring forth Jeremy's child.

Dwight arrived first, but not long behind him came Emma, riding pillion behind Matthew Mark. Demelza kissed Cuby and left the room. She wanted no part in it. She did not want to see her daughter-in-law in pain. Over the months the rapport between the two women had grown; Cuby told her sister she had never met a woman who understood her one half so well as Lady Poldark did; this understanding was almost though not entirely friendly and full of guarded but sincere affection. Perhaps in Demelza's reluctance to be near her daughter-in-law in childbirth lay the seeds of a fear that the hated sensations she had felt once were even yet not altogether vanquished.

Dwight was upstairs half an hour and then came into the parlour where Ross and Bella were playing a card game. Demelza was putting Henry to bed.

"All is very well," he said. "I see no complications."

"Perhaps we brought you out unduly," Ross said. "After leaving you so recent."

"No, no, it was the right thing to do. The contractions are mild and regular. I would think sometime tomorrow morning. Perhaps early."

"Your lead, Papa," said Bella.

"In the meantime?"

"In the meantime get a good night's sleep, as I propose to. I have given her a mild sedative, which should help, and Emma is now making her a cup of tea. Give my love to Demelza again."

"Of course." Ross led the ace of hearts.

"Emma will stay with her all night," Dwight said. "And have one of your boys close at hand and ready to come for me if there is any need."

"Your trick, Daddy," said Bella.

* * *

At five o'clock in the morning of St Stephen's Day Cuby Poldark was delivered of a healthy six-pound child. There were no complications, and, aware that she was in a strange house in spite of all the warmth and affection shown her, she gritted her teeth and bore the pain almost without a sound. Contrary to Ross's predictions, it was a girl. Dwight patted Cuby's hand and said she was very brave. The man who should have sat beside her bed and held her hand at this time was not there, and never would be. Through a mist of tears, part of happiness but more of sorrow, she was kissed and petted by each one of the family in turn. Henry laughed when he saw the baby. "Smaller'n me," he said. Despite Mrs Kemp's efforts, he affected a strong Cornish accent.

So there was another child in the house,

another Poldark, even if a girl; their first grand-child, Jeremy's daughter; another generation. A Christmas baby, a Christ child, all that was left of their soldier son.

About twelve Demelza said to Ross she would like to walk to the end of the beach, would he come with her?

"It's a long way for me," said Ross. "All that sand. Before I get home I shall be limping like Jago's donkey."

"Why don't we take our horses, then? Not for a gallop, just an amble."

"If you've the fancy I'll come."

"I've the fancy."

Colley and Marigold were both elderly and would not be restive at the thought of walking at a sedentary pace.

Demelza went upstairs for something, so Ross, while waiting for the horses to be brought round, went to his front door and stared over his land. This was where he belonged. The trees edged his view on the right, with the thin stream, copper stained and running under the bridge on its way towards Nampara Cove. The engine house and sheds of Wheal Grace half-way up the rising ground ahead of him; the piled attle spilling down towards the house, with rough weeds already growing over part of it (the two stamps had been gone some years, at Demelza's request — there were plenty in Sawle); his fields, mostly fallow, waited ploughing in February, speckled with crows seeking any scrap they could find; Demelza's walled garden with the gate leading to the beach, and the rough ground between the garden and the sand. Half a mile distant, on the first cliffs, the engine house and other buildings of Wheal Leisure.

And at his back the house, of nondescript architectural design, with its grey Delabole slate roof, except for a patch of thatch at the rear, its disparate chimneys, its thick granite walls, a house that had been put up by rough hands to meet the needs of the family it had sheltered for sixty years.

"I am ready," said Demelza as the horses came round.

They set off at a slow pace, the horses as companionable as the riders. Demelza carried a small canvas bag.

"What's in that?" Ross asked.

"Oh, something I just brought along with me."

It was half-tide, going out, and although there was no wind the sea was showing teeth at its edges. For a while they splashed through the surf, the horses relishing the water. Although the distant cliffs were black, those around Wheal Leisure had head cloths of green and feet of black and brown and purple seaweed. Over all was sky and cloud, ever changing. The scene-shifters were seldom idle in Cornwall.

"So we have a granddaughter," he said.

"Yes."

"Does that please you?"

"Yes, Ross. It pleases me."

"And Cuby?"

"And Cuby. I'm sure it pleases her too."

They rode on for a while.

Demelza said: "When she first came to Nampara — that first time — she seemed so composed, so assured, that I almost found it in me to mislike her. But very soon, within a day, I saw twas only a sort of shell. Under it she was soft, vulnerable, damaged, like a hurt animal with bloody and twisted paws . . . Can you imagine what it must be like to have your first child without a husband and among strangers?"

"Loving strangers."

"Oh yes. But if Jeremy had been here the sun would have lit the sky. She said to me the other day, she said, 'No one ever said my name like Jeremy. He has a special way of saying Cuby that was all his own . . . .'"

Tears were near, and there had been enough for Christmas. Ross said roughly: "And so this trumpery title I was so misguided as to accept will descend upon poor Henry."

"That pleases me too, Ross, except for your way of describing it. I believe it is more fitty that the honour should come to your own son."

They reached the drier sand.

"Has she given you any idea as to a name she may have in mind?"

"She thinks to call her Noelle. It seems that Jeremy suggested that. And Frances after her mother."

"Noelle Frances Poldark. It runs well enough. I'm glad she does not think of following the example of the Hornblower family."

"Hornblower?"

"Jonathan Hornblower, the man who invented

the compound engine; he died in March. His father had thirteen children and gave them all names beginning with J. Jeckolia, Jedediah, Jerusha, Josiah, Jabey, Jonathan. I have forgotten them. I used to know them all."

"You must tell Cuby. She may change her mind before christening day."

"On consideration," Ross said, "it is a pity that George did not have twin boys. Then he could have called them Castor and Pollux."

Demelza laughed. It was good to hear that sound again.

"Clowance would agree."

Ross looked over towards the land. "You see that sandhill? You remember how you and I and Jeremy and Clowance used to roll down it? It was a special treat when they were small."

"Too well," said Demelza. "It was a lovely time."

"I cannot imagine myself rolling down it with Harry."

"Don't worry. Noelle will."

Ross looped over his rein. "It is a strange feeling, but I do not think I shall ever *know* Harry the way I knew Jeremy. I am not likely to see so much of his life. The gap of the years between us . . . Sometimes I feel like his grandfather!"

"That is nonsense."

There wasn't another person to be seen; only the occasional congregation of gulls or sanderlings or plovers were disturbed by their approach, waddling out of their way, or flapping a lazy wing to increase the safe distance.

Demelza said: "I must send word to Clowance and Verity. I am sure they will be anxious to know."

"I'm sure they will."

"Ross, I have been wondering about Valentine and Selina in London."

"What could you be wondering about them?"

"Whether they may see Tom Guildford."

"You mean? . . . Oh my dear, it is too early to think of anything like that . . ."

"I do not think of anything like *that*! But Tom is a good kind friend of Clowance's. If he came down I am sure he would be good for Clowance, good for her spirits, good for her — her health generally. And do not forget, he is a lawyer. He could be a great business help to her too."

Ross said: "In that case perhaps we should send a note to Edward Fitzmaurice so the two gentlemen may start from scratch."

"Ross, you are *so* vexatious! Why do I bear with you?"

"Well, you said she told you that if she ever married again it would not be for love, it would be for money or position. That would bring Edward strongly into the reckoning."

"I do not know how you can be so cynical about your own daughter."

"Is it cynical to face the facts? If Cuby is damaged, so in a similar but different way is Clowance. So we should do nothing, should we, and allow events to take their course?"

They were half-way along the beach by now, past the old Wheal Vlow adit. The Dark Cliffs at the end were coming into perspective; you could see the deep crevices in them, the isolated rocks.

Demelza said: "And for yourself, Ross. Are you content?"

He was some seconds answering, his face devoid of readable expression.

"What is content? Something more than resignation? I eat and sleep well. I take interest in my affairs. I am content, more than content, with my wife."

"Thank you, Ross. I did not ask for a compliment."

"You did not get one. But — I have been home five months — you more. These have been months of grieving. But there is some slow adjustment. Do you not find it so?"

"Yes. And when Mr Canning calls to see us — if he calls to see us — what shall be your answer?"

"My answer to what? He has put no question."

"But he may do so. He is sure to try to persuade you back into public life."

"Then I shall not go."

"Really?"

"Really. I shall continue to look after my own property and my own still considerable family. And my wife, who is not quite considerable enough to please me."

"Oh, I am putting on weight, little by little. I am having to let out again some of the skirts that I took in."

"So you too are content?"

"Resigned? — that was the word you used.

260

That is nearer. But you are right: in time it will move by little stages farther away from grief."

"Perhaps even to happiness?"

"Ah *that* . . ."

"It is not in your nature, my dear, to be unhappy. You are in fine counterbalance with my natural mopishness."

"'Tis harder now," Demelza said.

They splashed through a pool of shallow water lying among corrugated ridges of sand.

"Old Tholly Tregirls," Ross said. "You know I went to see him just before he died? He said two things I have remembered. He quoted something my father said to him. My father said to him: 'Tholly, the longer I live, the more certain sure I am that the Wise Men never came from the East.'"

"I think he may be right."

"But something Old Tholly said himself made the deepest impression. It was only in passing. He did not mean it as a pronouncement. He said: 'A man is better off to be a squire in Cornwall than to be a king in England.'"

She looked across and he smiled back at her. He said: "Perhaps I have not always appreciated my good fortune."

★ ★ ★

Towards the end of the beach they dismounted and climbed up to the wishing well. It was really just a small natural circular pool at the entrance to a cave, with water dripping in plops from the moss-grown roof. It was a place where long ago

261

Drake and Morwenna had come with Geoffrey Charles and silently plighted their troth.

Ross had no idea why Demelza wanted to go there today, picking her way up with greater agility than he could muster among the pools and the sea-weedy rocks. But he went along, content to humour her. When they got to the well they stood for a moment in silence. The cave was in semi-darkness, though the day was bright around the well.

Demelza opened the canvas bag she carried, and took a small silver object out of it. It was the loving cup, bearing the Latin inscription, '*Amor gignit amorem*', 'Love creates love'.

Ross said: "Why have you brought that?"

"Cuby carried me a little note from Jeremy. It said — "

"You never told me — "

"Twas only a few words."

"You never told me. He did mention — in Belgium he did mention something that he had written to you."

"Twas only a note, Ross. It seems he had a sort of superstition about this cup. I cannot explain it any other way. I found it on the beach, you'll remember; it had been washed up by the sea. Jeremy thought it was an omen for him. If he came back from France he would take it as his own. If he did not I was to throw it back, give it back to the sea."

Ross frowned. "I don't understand. It was never his, was it? It doesn't make sense to me."

"It is not easy to understand how he felt, Ross.

But we talked about it once, when he was home last December. He didn't say as much then, but when Cuby came she brought this little note."

"I'd like to see the note."

"I have burned it, Ross."

Ross thought this so outrageous a lie that he could not dispute it. Demelza destroying any letter of Jeremy's . . .

"And now what are you going to do with this cup?"

"Drop it down the well."

"That is not the sea."

"To me it is better than the sea. And the well is quite deep. No one will ever find it."

"Is that important?"

"No. Oh no, not at all. But — this is a wishing well. I thought — I really thought it would be most fitty, most suitable."

"Well, it perplexes me, but have it as you will. Perhaps you have some Celtic perceptions that I lack."

"You are no less Cornish than I am, Ross."

"Maybe not. But sophistication has bred it out of me. Or your old Meggy Dawes taught you things only witches should know."

She smiled brilliantly at him, but there was no laughter in her eyes. She knelt on the stone beside the wall, rolled up her sleeve and put the cup slowly into the water. The cup filled, sent bubbles hurrying to the surface. She closed her eyes as if praying, opened her fingers. The cup sank out of sight. A few last bubbles rose and then it was gone.

It was as if with this symbolic action the ironic

tragedy of Jeremy's life and death, which even she could only partly perceive, had come full circle, had played itself out.

She remained kneeling for about a minute staring into the well. Then she got up, careful not to wipe her arm but to let the fresh water dry. When it had done so she pulled down her sleeve, buttoned it, and drew on her glove. Only then she looked up at her husband with eyes as dark as he had ever seen them.

"Dearest Ross, let us go home now. There is a baby to see to."

THE END

Other titles in the
Charnwood Library Series:

PAY ANY PRICE
Ted Allbeury

After the Kennedy killings the heat was on — on the Mafia, the KGB, the Cubans, and the FBI . . .

MY SWEET AUDRINA
Virginia Andrews

She wanted to be loved as much as the first Audrina, the sister who was perfect and beautiful — and dead.

PRIDE AND PREJUDICE
Jane Austen

Mr. Bennet's five eligible daughters will never inherit their father's money. The family fortunes are destined to pass to a cousin. Should one of the daughters marry him?

THE GLASS BLOWERS
Daphne Du Maurier

A novel about the author's forebears, the Bussons, which gives an unusual glimpse of the events that led up to the French Revolution, and of the Revolution itself.

CHINESE ALICE
Pat Barr
The story of Alice Greenwood gives a complete picture of late 19th century China.

UNCUT JADE
Pat Barr
In this sequel to CHINESE ALICE, Alice Greenwood finds herself widowed and alone in a turbulent China.

THE GRAND BABYLON HOTEL
Arnold Bennett
A romantic thriller set in an exclusive London Hotel at the turn of the century.

SINGING SPEARS
E. V. Thompson
Daniel Retallick, son of Josh and Miriam (from CHASE THE WIND) was growing up to manhood. This novel portrays his prime in Central Africa.

A HERITAGE OF SHADOWS
Madeleine Brent

This romantic novel, set in the 1890's, follows the fortunes of eighteen-year-old Hannah McLeod.

BARRINGTON'S WOMEN
Steven Cade

In order to prevent Norway's gold reserves falling into German hands in 1940, Charles Barrington was forced to hide them in Borgas, a remote mountain village.

THE PLAGUE
Albert Camus

The plague in question afflicted Oran in the 1940's.

THE RESTLESS SEA
E. V. Thompson

A tale of love and adventure set against a panorama of Cornwall in the early 1800's.

THE RIDDLE OF THE SANDS
Erskine Childers

First published in 1903 this thriller, deals with the discovery of a threatened invasion of England by a Continental power.

WHERE ARE THE CHILDREN?
Mary Higgins Clark

A novel of suspense set in peaceful Cape Cod.

KING RAT
James Clavell

Set in Changi, the most notorious Japanese POW camp in Asia.

THE BLACK VELVET GOWN
Catherine Cookson

There would be times when Riah Millican would regret that her late miner husband had learned to read and then shared his knowledge with his family.

THE WHIP
Catherine Cookson

Emma Molinero's dying father, a circus performer, sends her to live with an unknown English grandmother on a farm in Victorian Durham and to a life of misery.

SHANNON'S WAY
A. J. Cronin

Robert Shannon, a devoted scientist had no time for anything outside his laboratory. But Jean Law had other plans for him.

THE JADE ALLIANCE
Elizabeth Darrell

The story opens in 1905 in St. Petersburg with the Brusilov family swept up in the chaos of revolution.

THE DREAM TRADERS
E. V. Thompson

This saga, is set against the background of intrigue, greed and misery surrounding the Chinese opium trade in the late 1830s.

BERLIN GAME
Len Deighton

Bernard Samson had been behind a desk in Whitehall for five years when his bosses decided that he was the right man to slip into East Berlin.

HARD TIMES
Charles Dickens

Conveys with realism the repulsive aspect of a Lancashire manufacturing town during the 1850s.

THE RICE DRAGON
Emma Drummond

The story of Rupert Torrington and his bride Harriet, against a background of Hong Kong and Canton during the 1850s.

FIREFOX DOWN
Craig Thomas

The stolen Firefox — Russia's most advanced and deadly aircraft is crippled, but Gant is determined not to abandon it.

THE DOGS OF WAR
Frederic Forsyth

The discovery of the existence of a mountain of platinum in a remote African republic causes Sir James Manson to hire an army of trained mercenaries to topple the government of Zangaro.

THE DAYS OF WINTER
Cynthia Freeman

The story of a family caught between two world wars — a saga of pride and regret, of tears and joy.

REGENESIS
Alexander Fullerton

It's 1990. The crew of the US submarine ARKANSAS appear to be the only survivors of a nuclear holocaust.

SEA LEOPARD
Craig Thomas

HMS 'Proteus', the latest British nuclear submarine, is lured to a sinister rendezvous in the Barents Sea.

THE TORCH BEARERS
Alexander Fullerton

1942: Captain Nicholas Everard has to escort a big, slow convoy . . . a sacrificial convoy.

DAUGHTER OF THE HOUSE
Catherine Gaskin

An account of the destroying impact of love which is set among the tidal creeks and scattered cottages of the Essex Marshes.

FAMILY AFFAIRS
Catherine Gaskin

Born in Ireland in the Great Depression, the illegitimate daughter of a servant, Kelly Anderson's birthright was poverty and shame.

THE EXPLORERS
Vivian Stuart

The fourth novel in 'The Australians' series which continues the story of Australia from 1809 to 1813.

THE SUMMER OF THE SPANISH WOMAN
Catherine Gaskin

Clonmara — the wild, beautiful Irish estate in County Wicklow is a fitting home for the handsome, reckless Blodmore family.

THE TILSIT INHERITANCE
Catherine Gaskin

Ginny Tilsit had been raised on an island paradise in the Caribbean. She knew nothing of her family's bitter inheritance half the world away.

THE FINAL DIAGNOSIS
Arthur Hailey

Set in a busy American hospital, the story of a young pathologist and his efforts to restore the standards of a hospital controlled by an ageing, once brilliant doctor.

THE COLONISTS
Vivian Stuart

Sixth in 'The Australians' series, this novel opens in 1812 and covers the administration of General Sir Thomas Brisbane and General Ralph Darling.

IN HIGH PLACES
Arthur Hailey

The theme of this novel is a projected Act of Union between Canada and the United States in order that both should survive the effect of a possible nuclear war.

RED DRAGON
Thomas Harris

A ritual murderer is on the loose. Only one man can get inside that twisted mind — forensic expert, Will Graham.

CATCH-22
Joseph Heller

Anti-war novels are legion; this is a war novel that is anti-death, a comic savage tribute to those who aren't interested in dying.

THE ADVENTURERS
Vivian Stuart

The fifth in 'The Australians' series, opens in 1815 when two of its principal characters take part in the Battle of Waterloo.

THE SURVIVOR
James Herbert

David is the only survivor from an accident whose aftermath leaves a lingering sense of evil and menace in the quiet countryside.

LOST HORIZON
James Hilton

A small plane carrying four passengers crash-lands in the unexplored Tibetan wilderness.

THE TIME OF THE HUNTER'S MOON
Victoria Holt

When Cordelia Grant accepts an appointment to a girls' school in Devon, she does not anticipate anyone from her past re-emerging in her new life.

THURSTON HOUSE
Danielle Steel

At forty four, Jeremiah, a mining baron was marrying for the first time. Camille was a captivating eighteen-year-old girl. But can money buy happiness, a family . . . or love?

THE FOUNDER OF THE HOUSE
Naomi Jacob

The first volume of a family saga which begins in Vienna, and introduces Emmanuel Gollantz.

"THAT WILD LIE . . . "
Naomi Jacob

The second volume in the Gollantz saga begun with THE FOUNDER OF THE HOUSE.

IN A FAR COUNTRY
Adam Kennedy

Christine Wheatley knows she is going to marry Fred Deets, that is until she meets Roy Lavidge.

ONCE IN A LIFETIME
Danielle Steel

To the doctors the woman in the ambulance was just another casualty — more beautiful than most . . .